A
Harlequin
Romance

OTHER
Harlequin Romances
by MARY BURCHELL

Many of these titles are available at your local bookseller,
or through the Harlequin Reader Service.

For a free catalogue listing all available Harlequin Romances,
send your name and address to:

HARLEQUIN READER SERVICE,
M.P.O. Box 707, Niagara Falls, N.Y. 14302
Canadian address: Stratford, Ontario, Canada.

or use coupon at back of book.

STRANGERS
MAY MARRY

by

MARY BURCHELL

HARLEQUIN BOOKS   TORONTO
WINNIPEG

Original hard cover edition published
by Mills & Boon Limited.

SBN 373-01811-8

Harlequin edition published September 1974

CHAPTER 1

"GERALD says that's how life is," Susan explained impressively. "One person's good luck is bound to be someone else's bad luck."

Valerie looked gravely at her cousin and nodded – she hoped understandingly – in answer to this philosophical sentiment.

"He says he does see it's hard on you in a way, but then it isn't as though you were really Aunt Evelyn's daughter. He says blood *is* thicker than water, when all's said and done."

Valerie agreed mechanically that blood was indeed thicker than water.

"And then, as Gerald says, your being engaged to Larry makes a difference. It isn't as though you will *need* money when you're married."

Valerie supposed it was because she was still feeling weak and ill after the accident that she found it so difficult to enter into any discussion. As t was, instead of sharply condemning the implication that one could always sponge on a fiancé, she found she was simply wondering idly if Susan ever expressed an opinion which had not already been voiced by her husband first.

"Gerald says he doesn't want you to feel we're driving you *away*, of course, or anything like that." Susan's gaze wandered slightly now that she had reached the really

5

uncomfortable part of what Gerald had said. "But he's sure you'll see that –"

' – the really tactful thing would be for me to depart without being driven?" Valerie came to the surface suddenly, and completed Susan's sentence for her with what her cousin considered a very misplaced sense of humour.

"Oh, Val! You mustn't take it that way. Only, after all, poor Aunt Evelyn has been – I mean it *is* two months now since poor Aunt Evelyn passed away. And as she *didn't* leave any will and I *am* the only real relation – well, as Gerald says, one can't go against the law."

Valerie suppressed the unworthy reflection that probably Gerald would have been able to bring himself to go a little against the law if it would have been to his own advantage and he thought he would not be found out.

But, after all, that had nothing to do with the present situation. He and Susan were entirely within their rights – their legal rights. Susan *was* the sole blood relation of Aunt Evelyn. Valerie had only been her beloved adopted daughter for the last twelve years. And (to quote Gerald yet again) "there was nothing legal about that. Just an arrangement of sentiment and convenience."

"Well, Val?" Susan looked at her with an air of nervous expectancy that was both irritating and faintly pathetic. She was not a woman who enjoyed having trouble with anyone, but least of all did she relish trouble with Gerald.

Valerie got up from the long cane chair where she had been lying. To be able to walk again was still enough of a novelty to afford her active pleasure. Besides, it was dreadfully embarrassing to be contemplating anything but an unqualified "Yes" when Susan stared at one with those slightly prominent green eyes, and kept on putting back that loose strand of hair behind her right ear with a movement of nervous annoyance.

"Susan, I don't want in the least to impose on you and Gerald. It's – awfully good of you to have let me stay here these two months. But I - most of that time I was too ill to do any planning or thinking ahead, and" – Valerie found suddenly that she was at least as uncomfortable as Susan – "and, frankly, I'm only just getting used to the idea that I am without any money and without any home."

"Gerald said the best thing would be if Larry would marry you right away. Don't you think you could persuade him?" Susan suggested, with more enthusiasm than pride.

Two dashes of colour appeared in Valerie's cheeks, oddly accentuating their thinness.

"I don't imagine," she said coldly, "that I should have to do any 'persuading' where Larry was concerned. We hadn't meant to get married until he was through his finals, of course, and even then, probably not until he was settled in a job. But –"

"I daresay his mother would increase his allowance," Susan was beginning hopefully, when the door opened and Gerald came into the room.

"Well! Had a nice talk? Looking much better, I must say, Valerie."

Gerald – whose quite personable appearance was marred only by a certain thinness of the lips and narrow setting of the eyes – suffered from the delusion that by mutilating sentences one imparted an air of careless good-nature to one's conversation.

Valerie felt that "a nice talk" hardly covered her conversation with Susan. But Susan immediately said:

"Oh yes, Gerald."

"Fine. Said you'd be a sensible girl – see our point, Valerie."

Again Valerie felt ill-judged, though secret, amusement, for here was something "Gerald had said" which Susan had actually failed to report. Aloud she said:

"Yes, I do see your point, but –"

"Fine. I knew you would. Not that we want to turn you out. Feels quite like your own home after all these years, no doubt But we'd like to get my mother and my two sisters down to see us while the weather's still good. Must share one's good fortune, you know. Daresay Mrs Bowdon would be only too glad to put you up until you and Larry fix things. After all, it's only a case of acquiring her daughter-in-law a bit sooner."

But at this point Valerie felt bound to interrupt.

"I don't know that she would want to do that, Gerald. I certainly can't assume that she would. And as for this 'seeming like' home," she added, with a dangerous little blue flame of anger beginning to flicker in her eyes, "it not only seemed – it *was* my home."

"'Was' is the word," Gerald agreed smoothly, and his air of geniality dropped from him.

He added nothing to that meaning sentence – only clamped down his thin lips on the last word, as though nothing else should be allowed to escape from him for fear that, by some unforeseen chance, it should happen to be a kindly remark.

It was not easy to go on in the face of that, but Valerie did go on. She sat down on the side of the cane chair, however, because she found that her legs were trembling.

"Please don't think I'm cadging " She was unpleasantly aware that Gerald's narrow, unwinking grey eyes never left her face – "but this disaster did come on me out of the blue. No one could have – could have imagined Aunt Evelyn dying for another twenty years or more. I – I always thought of myself as having a safe and happy home behind me until I married. I only want you to know that I – that I must have a little time to adjust things and –"

"You mean you don't think Larry Bowdon will be so keen to marry you, now he knows your Aunt Evelyn hasn't left you anything? Well, better not say anything until –"

"How dare you!' Valerie sprang to her feet, unaware of any more trembling or weakness. "How dare you suggest that Larry is the same sort of – of money-grubbing skunk as yourself!"

She knew, of course, that she had gone much too far – even without Susan's frightened, "Val, Val!" to warn her.

A queer, angry brick-colour suffused Gerald's face, and his eyes seemed to grow even closer together.

"Now look here, Valerie, you'll not talk to me like that in my own house. And I'll thank you to remember that it *is* my house now –"

"Susan's, surely?" countered Valerie scornfully. But the interruption was brushed aside.

"*My* house," repeated Gerald, as though emphasis

might substantiate his claim. "You think that because Mrs. Hanson spoiled you and indulged you and made you forget you were a pauper and an orphan, that gives you a right to behave as though you were a real relation, but –"

"Isn't your own relationship a little far removed?" Valerie interrupted dryly, despising herself for allowing this undignified dispute, yet determined that Gerald should not swagger his way through everything while Susan stood by frightened and impressed.

"I happen to be married to Mrs. Hanson's only *real* relation," retorted Gerald with dignity. "You may have seen more of her than Susan did, but Susan is her real niece. Since Mrs. Hanson made no will, it's obvious that she intended her fortune to go to her own flesh and blood, and not to an unconnected upstart who served her no better than to kill her through her own carelessness."

"Oh – you – beast!" Valerie said quietly.

And then she said no more, because it seemed to her that her heart was rising in her throat to choke her – or perhaps it was just the terrible lump which came there every time she really let herself think of Aunt Evelyn. Aunt Evelyn who had been killed in that car smash when Valerie herself had been driving.

Gerald said nothing more either. Perhaps he felt that at last he had said enough.

As Valerie turned and went slowly from the room, Susan said in a frightened whisper, "Oh, Gerald!" – which was probably the strongest form of criticism she had ever ventured upon in her married life.

Gerald's reply was a somewhat pompous gesture demanding silence, and Susan – who had no intention of saying more in any case – pushed the inevitable strand of hair back behind her ear, and looked appropriately docile.

Valerie went upstairs to her own room – still slowly, but more because of a sort of blind bewilderment than real weakness.

That anyone – even Gerald – could have said such a cruel and wicked thing!

"Gerald says" – "Gerald would say" – "as Gerald said." The thousand and one banalities said by Gerald and faithfully chronicled by his wife hardly mattered now. What Gerald had said to her face was the only thing Valerie could remember.

He had said she had killed Aunt Evelyn with her carelessness.

It seemed almost unimportant that it was not true. The sheer statement gave substance at last to the incredible fact that *Aunt Evelyn was dead*. And, even if carelessness really had nothing to do with the accident, it was still true that it was Valerie's lack of skill or lack of judgment or just sheer bad luck which had killed her.

"I was the instrument," thought Valerie with a sort of horror. "Nothing can change that."

Feverishly she wrenched open the door of her wardrobe and took out a coat at random.

She must go to Larry. Larry would understand and comfort her. Thank God she had him! Not to cadge from and deceive as Gerald and Susan so earnestly advised. But just to speak to. She must feel the comforting pressure of his arms, know that someone – the only person in the world who mattered now that Aunt Evelyn had gone – someone loved her and cared what happened to her.

She pulled on her coat – a soft powder blue coat which, like so many of her prettiest things, had been a present from Aunt Evelyn. Twisting a blue scarf round her smoky-dark hair, she glanced automatically in the mirror, but she really hardly noticed the reflection of the slim, dark-haired girl with the blue eyes that seemed a little too big because of the shadows round them.

She only thought subconsciously – "How dreadfully thin my face is. I suppose it's having been ill so long. But oh, what right had I to be only injured when Aunt Evelyn was killed outright?"

Susan and Gerald gave no sign of having heard her when she came downstairs. But as Valerie went down the garden path, two pairs of eyes observed her with great interest from the window of the lounge.

"Oh dear! she hasn't got any luggage with her," sighed Susan – because she really had hoped that the whole unpleasant business was over and done with.

"Don't be a fool," retorted her husband amiably. "She's gone to talk it over with him. She can always send for her luggage afterwards."

Unaware of the speculation behind her, Valerie went along the short drive from Monks Alder, past the high straight trees which gave the house its name, and out into the lane beyond.

Every inch of the way was dear and familiar to her, for, as she had told Gerald, Monks Alder had not only seemed like her home – it had *been* her most dearly loved home for twelve happy years.

Even now she could remember quite clearly the first

day she had come here – not as a decorous guest along the drive, but as a skinny, dark-haired little girl who had played truant from the near-by children's home, and pushed her way through the hedge to gaze in spellbound wonder at the water-lilies on the pool in the garden.

She had known nothing about Monks Alder then – had no idea that it had just passed into new ownership, and that the villagers of Arden were informing each other with a pleasurable sense of shock that "Mrs. Hanson was one of those ladies that talk to all and sundry like. Not county, you understand – something to do with the stage, they say – but nice, mind you."

It was by the lily-pond that Aunt Evelyn had found her – not touching anything, just gazing with those great blue eyes that were even then too large for her little white face.

"Aren't they lovely?" Aunt Evelyn had said.

Not, "What are you doing here?" or "Run away!" or "Don't you know you aren't allowed here?" Just – "Aren't they lovely?"

And Valerie had said rather huskily:

"Yes. Are they real?"

"Quite real." Aunt Evelyn had laughed. "Give me your hand, and then you can lean over and touch one, just to see for yourself."

A little shyly Valerie had put a thin, grubby hand into Aunt Evelyn's, and leant over to touch a lily-cup with great tenderness.

"Thank you," she said gravely when the operation was over. And then Aunt Evelyn had asked her to stay to tea.

It had been awkward, of course, when one had really been running away from the home. But, at the same time, it might be a good idea to set out into the world with a good meal inside one.

So Valerie had stayed to tea, and somehow had found herself explaining about running away.

Aunt Evelyn had not been shocked or said how wicked she was. She simply looked reflective and said:

"But do you think it's a very good idea? It will be awfully cold wandering about in the winter, don't you think?"

Valerie hadn't thought of that. She scuffled her feet a little and muttered that she hated the home.

Aunt Evelyn had nodded sympathetically.

"I know. There's always something in your life that you simply detest. But the funny thing is that nearly always, just as you think you can't stand it any longer, something happens which makes it seem much better. For instance, if you *had* been staying, instead of going away, I daresay you would have liked to come here to tea with me once a week. It seems a pity. But then, if you're quite determined to go –"

In the long pause which followed that, Valerie had slowly digested the new suggestion.

"I daren't go back now," she said finally. "They'd be so mad with me."

"Not if I took you back and explained, I think," Aunt Evelyn had said pleasantly.

And so, in the end, Valerie had not run away after all. Aunt Evelyn took her back to the home, miraculously saved her from being even scolded, and arranged that every Sunday in future she should come to tea at Monks Alder.

From that day life had changed. The Sunday visits remained a regular institution; but, as often as not, Valerie went to Monks Alder twice and even three times in the week.

Then a year later, when the home had been moved to another part of the country, Valerie had remained behind at Monks Alder.

There was no need for her to leave the home. The home left her. And with it went every vestige of feeling that she was a foundling or a "charity child." The enlightened authorities at the home allowed Mrs. Hanson to become her official foster-mother. Though she called Mrs Hanson "Aunt Evelyn," their relationship was very much more that of mother and daughter. Life had become a secure and happy and wonderful thing.

Valerie paused in her walk, on the crest of a gently sloping green hill, and looked back at Monks Alder, friendly and mellow in the evening sunlight.

It was a beautiful old house – not large, but full of personality, and set in grounds on which generations must have lavished loving care. Only so did one achieve such unconventional riot of colour in the wide flower borders, such deep green shade of ancient trees, such careless profusion in the well-stocked kitchen garden.

Local legend had it that the land around had once been the grounds of a monastery. But there was nothing to show that now, except the name of the house, and a deep well in the far corner of the grounds, of which the villagers used to say positively, "That'd be where the monks got their water."

"Why, hello, Miss Valerie!"

Recalled suddenly to the present, Valerie turned quickly to greet the old village doctor who had come up behind her.

"Hello, Doctor Anderton." Valerie smiled her pleasure, for the doctor was an old friend, and one of the few people who knew the exact circumstances of her coming to Aunt Evelyn.

"Taking an evening stroll, eh? Well, there's no harm in that if you don't go far. But I daresay you're not going any farther than a certain young man's house." And the doctor laughed.

"No, I promise not to go far. Only it's such a lovely evening, and –" She glanced back at Monks Alder without completing the sentence, but perhaps her expression did that for her.

"I know, I know." A slightly worried look came over the doctor's kindly face. "Home isn't quite home with strangers there."

"Well, Susan isn't exactly a stranger, of course. She often stayed with us. Only" – Valerie gave a nervous little laugh – "in a way, it's I who am the visitor now. It's not quite easy to realise it."

She saw this was by no means news to the doctor, and he shook his head.

"Well, you'll have to try to feel it is still home until Larry gets through those exams of his and you set up your own home together. A year should see him through now. But I can understand that the situation isn't exactly an easy one for you."

Valerie could not tell him that her boats were, in fact,

already burnt – or, at any rate, about to burst into flame. But, on impulse, she said:

"I think I shall get a job, Doctor. I can't impose on Susan and Gerald, you know. These are uncertain times, and no one wants the extra responsibility of –"

"Nonsense, my dear." The doctor was quite emphatic. "There's no question of imposing. Everyone knows it was a great surprise to your cousin and her husband when they inherited Mrs. Hanson's money. There isn't any doubt that she intended you to have most of it, only unfortunately, like a lot of unwise people, she left the making of her will too late. She couldn't know, poor lady, of course –" The doctor paused to shake his head again over the mingled bad luck and bad management of it all. Then he went on almost immediately, "The least your cousin can do is to let you stay on in your own home until you are married."

"I think, all the same," Valerie said gently but obstinately, "that I would rather try to get a job and be independent. After all, there are heaps of jobs going, and –"

But Doctor Anderton interrupted quite sharply.

"I'm afraid I must be quite firm about that, my dear. You can't possibly take any sort of job that would entail hard or regular work. You have to be very careful indeed for the next six months or a year, or you will have serious trouble with that injury to your spine."

"But" – Valerie, too, spoke sharply in her fear and dismay – "I thought I was getting well so wonderfully – that I was really convalescent now."

"So you are," the doctor assured her. "But you mustn't take liberties with your health for a long while.

There is nothing to cause alarm, and you're doing very well indeed. But there is no harm in telling you now that you're a lucky girl to be alive on this nice evening. You very nearly were not, you know."

For a moment Valerie thought bitterly that "lucky" was hardly the word. It would have been simpler to have been dead, like poor Aunt Evelyn – quickly and without knowing anything – right away from all these dreadful problems.

But the next moment she was ashamed of herself for the cowardice of her thoughts.

Besides, there was Larry. *He* would think of some way out of this tangle. Nothing would seem so bad when she had talked things over with him.

Valerie managed to smile at Dr. Anderton.

"Well, if you're quite determined that I shall be a useless parasite for the next year, what can I say?"

"Don't use such absurd words!" The doctor sounded genuinely annoyed. "Anyone can have the misfortune to meet with an accident, and I am sure your cousin will be generous enough to you out of this unexpected wealth of hers."

He was not at all sure, of course. He didn't think generosity was the outstanding characteristic of the spineless, unimaginative Mrs. Manders. And as for that thin-lipped husband of hers –!

But what else could one say to this poor child who was obviously scared and bewildered by her position, in spite of her determined smile? One could only hope that the cousin and her husband would be shamed into doing something for her, even if they would not act from any worthier motive.

Valerie said good-bye to the doctor then, and went on her way. It was not far now. Down the side lane – past the big oak where she and Larry had sheltered from the rain that day they got engaged. The moment she saw him everything would be all right.

And then she did see him – coming towards her, with a step which quickened immediately when he saw her.

"Why, Val! This is wonderful. It's the first time you've come so far, isn't it?"

"Yes. I – wanted most awfully to see you." She thankfully took his arm, leaning on it just a little, for she found suddenly that she was more tired than she had realised. "Where can we go and talk?"

"Why, come along in, of course. Mother is out."

There was no deliberate meaning in the way that was put, but, as a matter of fact, Valerie knew quite well that there was an unconscious significance in it. Mrs. Bowdon had never been known to express any warm approval of her son's choice of a wife. And Valerie, as well as Larry, felt that her being out at this moment was an advantage.

They went rather slowly towards the house.

Mrs. Bowdon's choice of a home differed very much from that of Aunt Evelyn. Like herself, it was elegant, even beautiful, but always slightly cold. No one ever sat on the rug in front of her fire, or went into the kitchen to make cocoa at night, or made an impromptu meal out of tins, with everyone talking at once and waiting on themselves.

"I see no point in doing a thing at all unless one can do it properly," she was fond of saying, and possibly this theory accounted for her coolness and lack of enthusiasm about her son's engagement. For, though everyone else might accept Valerie more or less as Mrs. Hanson's daughter, the real situation was something rather different – different enough for Mrs. Bowdon to consider her at heart not quite the perfect wife for her son. And, if Larry could not choose the perfect match as his wife, was it not better for him not to choose one at all?

No one had ever heard Mrs. Bowdon express herself in so many words – she was too careful to be the perfect mother for that – but Valerie was not so insensitive as to be unaware that strong, unknown currents ran just below the smooth surface of Mrs. Bowdon's irreproachable manner towards herself.

The room into which Larry brought her now was furnished very tastefully in modern style, and it had french windows which looked out on to a formal, perfectly kept garden.

"Oh, that's nice, Larry." Valerie smiled at him as he put her into a deep armchair by the window. She was tired now and glad to be able to sit down and relax – mentally as well as physically.

"Sherry?" Larry wanted to know. "Or shall I get Jane to make coffee?"

"Oh no, thank you."

"Will you have another cushion, Val? Here – take this one!"

"No, really, I'm all right." Valerie laughed a little protestingly. "Just sit down, darling, and let's talk."

"Well, one moment while I draw the curtain a little. The sun is in your eyes."

"I'm all right." Valerie felt the slightest edge of irritation sawing at her nerves. Was she imagining things about everyone this evening, or was Larry really restless and slightly ill at ease?

The idea was absurd. But she wished he would sit quiet and just let her look at him.

"I'm very comfortable now, thanks." She smiled at him because she felt remorseful about her secret irritation.

"That's good." He lounged against the side of the french window, his hands in his pockets, his eyes momentarily busy with something in the garden.

She wished he would look at her. But then she was just being a silly, peevish invalid to make a point of anything like that. She must pull herself together!

How very dear Larry was. Even in repose, as he was for the moment, he looked full of energy – ready to start up on impulse and suggest some pleasant, crazy plan. No one else had the same bright, fair hair which seemed to stand up from his forehead with the sheer force of the vitality in him. And, even before she fell in love with him, she had always liked the way his nice square chin was slightly cleft, in a way that gave an oddly attractive touch of boyishness to his whole face.

She had once heard it said that men with cleft chins were apt to be unreliable. What silly things people said, and how stupid generalisations were!

Larry turned his head then and smiled at her. He was going to say something, but, before he could speak, she tackled the real subject in hand.

"Larry, I've more or less had my marching orders from Susan and Gerald." She managed to laugh about it as she said it, but it was a small laugh and rather uncertain.

"You've – what, Val? The skunks! Oh, but they'll get over it. What happened? Their dignity upset about something?"

He came and leant on the back of her chair – solicitously, but somehow she would rather have had him where she could see his expression.

"No, it's more serious than that. They're delighted, of course, with the idea of owning Monks Alder, but they don't quite see why they should give house-room to a poor relation who isn't even a real relation. Susan tried to be tactful about it, but after she had gone round and round the point, Gerald came in and took a hand. He said – he said – oh, Larry! – the most awful things. I feel I can't ever go back there! They've spoilt everything. To think of them in dear Monks Alder! Oh, it's no good thinking about it. It's all over now."

"What's all over?" There was the deepest concern in Larry's voice.

"Oh, all the good days there, I suppose I meant. It's the end of a chapter in my life, and I'm finding it hard to realise the fact." Valerie turned in her chair and smiled up at him, but without any real amusement.

Larry looked very grave.

"Poor little Val. It's rotten for you. They never have been exactly cordial, have they?"

"No. I suppose it was a sort of jealousy."

"Probably. And jealousy is confoundedly hard to live with."

Valerie nodded.

"What are you going to do about it? I mean – will you try to patch things up? – or are you thinking of cutting loose and starting on your own?"

22

"Well, it's a bit difficult to decide just *how* to start on my own with nothing but the remnants of my last quarter's allowance," Valerie explained.

"I see." Larry frowned thoughtfully. "There *are* plenty of jobs going, of course, but you don't want just anything. Are things too strained for you to ask Gerald to help you to find something? He's probably got all sorts of contacts."

"Well, you see –" Valerie stopped. She had been going to explain about Doctor Anderton's forbidding her to work, when suddenly an unpleasant little chill held her silent. Was it only her imagination that Larry seemed more worried than resourceful in this emergency? Certainly it had not entered his head that they should hasten on their marriage.

She could hardly say anything herself – or could she? After all, it was absurd if two people who loved each other could not be perfectly frank in a crisis which concerned them both.

"Larry" – again she twisted round so that she could look up into his face – "you don't think the solution might be for us to get married sooner than we intended?"

She saw immediately that, for some reason, the idea slightly startled him.

"I don't quite see how we could, Val. Not until I'm through my finals. We couldn't very well pig it in some pokey two-room flat."

"I – I know in the ordinary way it would be unpractical. Only – Larry, I'm really without a home and Dr. Alnderton says –"

"Oh, come, Val dear! It isn't quite as bad as all that.

I'm sure it was rotten for you, and I think Susan and her Gerald are poisonous, but I daresay your not being well made things seem worse than they were. You'll feel a whole lot better in the morning."

"Oh no, it isn't like that at all." Valerie looked at him rather wonderingly. Was it possible that Larry – *Larry* – didn't understand? Or was it just that she had ventured to suggest something outside practical possibilities and it made him unhappy and touchy that he could not give it to her?

She touched the hand which rested on the back of her chair – hardly aware of her own nervousness expressed in the movement.

"I wouldn't have suggested it, dear, only – I'm worried. You see, they do just intend to turn me out, and –"

"They can't do that." Larry was positive.

"Well, not literally push me out of the front door, of course. But they *have* asked me to go – and quite unmistakably too."

Larry muttered something which was presumably his private opinion of Susan and Gerald.

"Is it – quite – impossible? Our marrying now, I mean. I'm a good manager, Larry, and we shouldn't mind having things very simple at first, should we?"

"It's impossible, Val." The unfamiliar curtness of that made Valerie feel suddenly that she had been cheap and pushing even to make the suggestion. Yet how could she do otherwise? She and Larry had always discussed their plans and their pleasures down to the last detail. Whom else should she consult, if not Larry?

Perhaps her silence told Larry that he had been too short with her. Worriedly he amplified his statement.

"I have absolutely nothing but my grant, remember."

Valerie felt she could not remind him at this moment that the grant would be increased if he got married. But, as though he had read her thoughts, he added:

"Mother could help out, of course. But it's entirely dependent on her decision."

For a moment Valerie failed to take in the implication of that. Then she whitened slightly, and her voice, when she spoke, had gone flat and cold.

"You mean – your mother doesn't really want you to marry me at all?"

"Oh, Val, I didn't say that."

"But you were thinking it."

Larry thrust his hands into his pockets and moved away to the window again.

With something like shock, Valerie realised that he was curiously ill at ease. She had never seen him like that before, and somehow the discovery shook her more than anything else that had happened that evening.

"Larry, you aren't being quite frank with me, are you?" She spoke gently, but with a certain urgency in her tone which made him protest at once.

"Oh, nonsense, Val dear. You're just fanciful. You mustn't go imagining things about Mother like that. Only it's quite true that she wouldn't like the idea of our marrying right away. And the brutal fact is that, since she does hold the purse-strings, she naturally has the last word."

"You mean she would refuse to help you financially if you married me?" Valerie's voice had gone strangely cold again. "How she must dislike me."

"She doesn't, Val! Only she just wouldn't counten-

25

ance an immediate marriage. As it is – well, anyway, she wouldn't have it.''

"As it is –? What were you going to say?''

"Oh, nothing.'' Larry sounded impatient and put out.

"As it is, there is already something about the engagement which she dislikes? What is it, Larry?''

For a moment she thought he was not going to answer her. Then he came over to her and stood looking down moodily at her.

"Look here, Val, you mustn't be hurt about it. But there's been a lot of talk in the village since the accident, of course, and Mother is upset because it's come out somehow about your being an orphan, and –''

"But she always knew I wasn't Aunt Evelyn's daughter!''

"Yes, yes, I know. But she imagined you were the daughter of an old friend or a relation or something. Some wretched old village cat has been spilling the story to her, I suppose. You know what Mother is. She's a darling, but she's a bit of a snob. And the idea that the orphanage was actually here at one time made a difference too, no doubt.''

Valerie could not help wondering why it should, but aloud she said :

"And does it make a difference with you, too, Larry?''

"Val, that isn't fair!''

"I don't know why not. There's no reason why you should feel differently from your mother. It's quite true – I am an orphan. If Aunt Evelyn hadn't taken me I should probably have been brought up to work in a shop. That's what your mother doesn't like, isn't it? That and the fact that, as I'm no real relation to Aunt

Evelyn, I don't inherit Monks Alder or her money. *That's* what makes the difference, Larry. And I think it makes a difference to you as well as to your mother."

If she had been less upset she would have hesitated before voicing the sudden suspicion which welled up in her heart. As it was, it seemed to her that Larry – like every other pillar of her familiar life – was failing her, and the discovery frightened and stung her beyond expression.

At any other time she would have made excuses for him – tried to see the difficulties of his position. But at the moment she was too scared to see anything but her own terrifying dilemma. She only knew that his words carried no conviction as he eagerly protested:

"Val, I don't know how you can say such a thing to me!"

"Because it's true, that's all. It would be unpardonable if it were not true, but you just don't want to marry a girl who can't bring you any money. Perhaps you're no worse than lots of other men for that – perhaps you have to have the luxuries of life or else you can't be happy. Only I don't happen to be any good to that sort of man, for the simple reason that I haven't a bean."

"Val, will you stop trying to make me sound like some damned fortune-hunter!" Larry, too, was white and angry now. "I'm nothing of the sort, only –"

"Only the money does make a difference, doesn't it?"

"Of course it makes a difference," he retorted with angry candour. "Money always makes a difference. If your aunt had left you her money you wouldn't have been in this confounded hole now. But that doesn't mean I was marrying you because I thought you were

27

an heiress, as you seem to want to make out."

She made a great effort to regain control of herself, though the vehemence of Larry's protests allied to the curious fact that he never categorically denied her charge made her more frightened than she would have believed possible.

"I – didn't mean to suggest that, Larry. Only I think it means a good deal to you to find yourself engaged to a girl who started life in a children's home instead of a girl who was an heiress in a small way."

"Val, won't you understand that it's Mother who takes objection to these things?"

"And your mother's opinion means a great deal to you, doesn't it?"

"Well, of course." Larry spoke with unaccustomed stiffness. "You know perfectly well that I think the world of her."

Valerie was silent for a moment, trying not to remember that she had once supposed he thought the world of her.

After a short pause, Larry said anxiously:

"You do see, Val, don't you, that it wouldn't do for us to get married right away?"

"Oh – yes, of course." Valerie spoke almost absently, because somehow that had all become quite a minor part of the problem. "I think I see something else, too, Larry," she added slowly and rather deliberately. "That it wouldn't really do for us to get married at all."

Until she drew her ring from her finger and held it out to him, he didn't seem to realise what she meant. Then he drew back sharply.

"No, Val! You can't be as angry as that!"

"I'm not angry." And as she said that, she realised it was true. She was not angry any more. Only chilled and determined and rather agonisingly disillusioned.

"Then why do you want to give me back your ring?"

"Because I don't see how we could make a success of things now, Larry. If everything had gone smoothly, we – we should have been all right together. We should never have been tested and never found each other's weaknesses. But as it is, I don't think you'd enjoy our life together somehow unless we both had money, and I don't think I should be a success as your mother's daughter-in-law. Maybe it's unreasonable of me, but I'm afraid I should expect to come first with you – and I've a feeling she would expect to do the same."

"Val" – Larry was eagerly appealing now – "won't you give things more of a chance? Wait and see if Mother changes her mind."

Valerie flushed slightly.

"No, thank you. I have got a little pride, you know, even if I did start life in a home. I think I – I've been on approval quite long enough. As I don't attach so much importance to your mother's approval as you do, I don't feel inclined to – to hang about on the chance of attaining it one day."

Larry bit his lip – but whether with anger or indecision Valerie could not tell. If only at that moment he would have snatched her up in his arms, reassured her, told her she meant more than anything else in the world to him! But the moment lengthened and the opportunity passed.

He looked desperately unhappy, but she noticed too that his glance wandered to the handsome photograph of his mother which seemed somehow to dominate the room.

It was that glance which finally decided Valerie.

Placing her ring on the table, since it seemed impossible to make him take it, she spoke quietly, almost gently.

"I'm not going to say anything silly like 'Well, this is good-bye,' but I think I'll go now, Larry."

"Val, you haven't told me what you're going to do. About Susan and Gerald – or getting a job, I mean."

"I'll manage all right. Don't worry."

"But I can't let you go like that!"

"You haven't really any choice, have you?" she said quietly.

"But I want to know what your plans are."

"I haven't any. I'll make them tomorrow. But you needn't be anxious. I – I can look after myself."

"Val, you'll let me know what you decide to do, won't you?"

"I expect so."

"Won't you even let me see you home now?"

"No, thank you, Larry. I think that would be very embarrassing for us both, and not specially dignified, don't you?"

"I don't know that embarrassment matters much at a moment like this," Larry said unhappily. "Or dignity, either, come to that."

"I think dignity always matters," Valerie said. And she went out of the room and out of the house without even waiting for him to open the door for her.

Until she was out of sight of the house, Valerie walked

quickly, her figure erect and her head held high. If Larry were looking from the window, he should not have any impression that she went out of his life drooping.

But as soon as possible she turned aside through a small gate into a pine wood, for she felt she could not go home by the road and risk meeting someone.

She could not go home at all, come to that, because there was really no home to go to. Only a house where she was very unwelcome.

For the first time, great waves of uncontrollable panic overwhelmed her. What *was* she to do? Aunt Evelyn had gone. Larry had gone. Her health and her earning capacity had gone, at any rate for the time. She had been staving off these inescapable facts until now, but at last they had caught up with her, and she had to turn and face them.

But she could not face them.

Suddenly she began to run, as though she would literally run away from them again. She wanted to reach the depths of the wood and somehow hide her fear and shame and despair.

It made her feel dreadfully weak to run like that, but she didn't care. She would run and run until –

She hardly knew what it was that caught her foot. A stone – a root hidden in the soft carpet of pine needles, perhaps. But, whatever it was, it tripped her and sent her falling headlong.

For a moment the shock made everything go blank. Then, as though it had suddenly snapped some tremendous tension, the tears began to run down her cheeks. She was powerless to stop them – powerless even to get up again. She could only lie there among the pine

31

needles, with her head on her arms, crying and crying for her broken world and her lost happiness.

Valerie had no idea how long she had lain there, with nothing but the sound of her own sobs and the soft sigh of the breeze through the pine-trees, when suddenly another sound broke the stillness. A man's voice – deep, unfamiliar, and with the faintest drawl in it.

"Oh, come – nothing on earth is worth a flood like that. It doesn't help whatever is wrong, and it's probably making a perfect fright of you. Why don't you get up and look at life from a different angle?"

CHAPTER II

WITH a slight gasp, Valerie sat up, pushing back the hair from her forehead.

She was ashamed that anyone should find her like this, and afraid for a moment that, in spite of the unfamiliarity of the voice, it was someone she knew.

But she had never seen the man who was looking down at her now. A tall, dark, loose-limbed man who was leaning negligently against a pine-tree, rather as though he might have been there some time studying her. There was a slight smile on his lips, and his eyes, though cynical, were not unkindly. They suggested that he had seen most things, thought little of nearly all of them, but retained an amused expectation of one day seeing something worth while.

"What is the matter?" He didn't move from his position as he spoke again. "Has the only man in the world let you down?"

Valerie stared at him for a moment, surprised perhaps at his penetration or his shrewd guess. Then –

"It isn't – only that," she said at last.

"A variety of evils, eh? But don't you think they'll look a bit less dreadful if you take them home, instead of crying about them in a wood, with night coming on?"

She glanced down at her ringless hands, locked together now in her lap, and out of the depths of her misery she said:

"I haven't got a home."

He must have thought that savoured of self-pity, because his heavy dark eyebrows lifted incredulously.

"Hm – a friendless orphan? – in that coat?" And he glanced with speculative amusement over her expensive blue coat.

Valerie glanced at the coat too. Then the faintest smile lit up her face – a flicker of genuine amusement, in spite of everything.

"Well, an ex-orphan – about to revert to type – would really describe it better," she admitted.

He laughed then, and she saw what magnificent teeth he had – very square and white against the dark tan of his skin. As he straightened up, she saw how tall he was too, and when he came and sat on the ground beside her, she was irresistibly reminded of a very fine, healthy animal – willing to be friendly, but reserving the right to bound away – or stay and fight things out – just as he chose.

"Are you going to tell me what is really wrong?" He looked at her with a sort of naïve curiosity, which belied the wisdom of his eyes and yet was entirely inoffensive.

With instinctive reserve Valerie said:

"Why should I? I don't even know who you are."

"Well, I don't know who you are," he pointed out carelessly. "So we're quits there."

She smiled again at that. And then was aware of a curious and intense desire to tell him – tell *some*one. She wanted to hear some sort of comment other than the comment of her own wretched thoughts and fears.

"I daresay it isn't so very unusual and tragic." she said slowly. "Only, when it happens to oneself –" She broke off with a sigh, and he nodded.

"Yes, I know. Tragedy is what happens to oneself. Drama is what happens to the other fellow."

Again that faint smile touched Valerie's lips.

"Isn't that a bit self-centred?"

"Maybe," he agreed indifferently. "But it's human nature."

"Well – all right. We'll leave it at that. Then perhaps I'm only being human in supposing it is a tragedy because I've lost my home, my – my fiancé, and, to a certain extent, my health."

"Whew! That's a good deal to say good-bye to all at once." He glanced at her again with that oddly inoffensive curiosity. "I thought you looked a delicate little thing," he remarked candidly. "That's one reason why you ought to be going ho – Well, anyway, not staying out much longer."

"Yes, I know. I didn't really mean that I was without a roof over my head tonight. Only what was once my home – such a beautiful home – has now gone to relations who don't want me there any longer and have said so pretty plainly."

"Have your parents just died, then?"

"No. My guardian."

"Oh – your guardian? Yes, of course – that's where the orphan bit comes in. And he left everything away from you?"

"She – not he. And she didn't do anything like that deliberately. She was the dearest, kindest woman who ever breathed. She was – killed in an accident, years before she could ever have thought of – dying. There

35

was no will and everything goes automatically to a niece of hers."

"And the niece has cut up rough about doing anything for you?"

"It's more her husband than she herself." Valerie made an honest attempt to believe that, left to herself, Susan would have been more generous. "Anyway, of course, there isn't any reason why they should support me indefinitely. I didn't think of anything like that. Only I was – I was injured in the accident too, and the doctor says –" She stopped suddenly. "Oh, but do you really want to hear all this?"

"I do. Go on. What does the doctor say?"

"That I can't work for my own living for six months anyway – perhaps a year. It leaves me – rather stranded. And then my engagement is broken too. It seemed like everything together, you know. I don't often cry in that idiotic way. It was just – everything," she repeated a little forlornly.

"Did he break it off because of – Oh well, I suppose that really isn't my business."

"No, it isn't," Valerie agreed, wondering why she had told him so much.

He grinned, quite unabashed, and a little contritely she added, "But it was kind of you to listen to my sad tale, all the same."

"Not at all. I was interested. I suppose you are Mrs. Hanson's little girl?"

Valerie glanced at him in astonishment – partly because of the description of herself.

"Yes. But how did you know? I thought you were a stranger here."

"So I am. At least, it's under twenty-four hours since I arrived at the village inn. But Arden's as good a place for gossip as any other village, and I heard about the accident."

"Oh." She felt faintly uncomfortable now. When neither had known who the other was there had been a reassuring sort of impersonality about telling him everything. That he should know who she was rather altered things.

Reluctantly her mind moved away from the present to the immediate future. She must go back to Monks Alder. There was nowhere else to go, and Susan and Gerald would be wondering what had happened to her. Indeed, they were probably already congratulating themselves on the fact that it seemed she was not coming back.

Too bad to disappoint them, thought Valerie, with a flash of grim humour, but that could not be helped.

She turned her head and smiled slightly at the man whose unexpected kindness and impersonal type of sympathy had somehow steadied her and made her feel she could go on with life again.

"I'll have to go now."

As she moved to stand up, he took her hand and helped her to her feet. Only then did she quite realise how weak she felt. Just for a moment she clung to his arm, and immediately he said:

"What is it? Have you hurt yourself?"

"No – no. It's just that I feel rather – weak. It was the fall, I expect."

"When did you fall? Just now?" He looked concerned.

"Yes. I tripped over something. That was what made me start cr – At least, that was what seemed the finishing touch."

"You'd better let me carry you," he said.

"Oh *no*! It's quite a long way."

"Well, you're only a snip of a thing." He smiled at that, and she saw that his peculiarly light hazel eyes looked amused out of all proportion to the occasion.

"If you don't mind giving me your arm –" she said a little diffidently.

"Not at all," he assured her, still with that amusement, as though he were indulging her, and genuinely enjoyed doing so.

But after a few yards he took the matter out of her hands.

"Look here, you can't manage this way," and, picking her up off the ground, he set off along the path through the trees, adding, "You'll have to tell me which way to go when we get to the end here."

Valerie was slightly embarrassed in spite of her relief. Being carried by a strange man seemed the last touch of absurdity in a pretty trying evening.

"I'm afraid it really is a long way," she said. "I think I *could* have managed."

"No, you couldn't. And anyway – I've told you – you're only a snip of a thing. I can 'manage' a great deal better than you can."

"Well – thank you very much. It's nice of you to make so little of it. I've always thought it's nothing but a romantic fiction that a man can go lugging a girl about the countryside without noticing it, however small she may be."

38

Glancing up into his dark face, she saw the amused flash of his teeth again.

"All right. When I start gasping and the perspiration runs down me, you can argue again," he said.

Valerie found that she too could laugh then. And certainly he carried her all the way to the back of Monks Alder without any signs of acute distress.

"Will you put me down here, please? It's just the edge of the garden, and if I go through this wicket gate I have only a few yards more."

"Sure you will be all right?"

"Quite sure, thank you. I'm sorry I can't ask you in, but – well, you understand."

"Yes, I understand." He glanced rather curiously, she thought, through the trees and the deepening dusk. "So that's Monks Alder? It's a pretty house."

"It's the loveliest house in the world, I think," Valerie said with a sigh.

"Well, cheer up." He smiled as he took the hand she held out to him. "Perhaps things won't be so bad as you think."

She thought he didn't know Susan and Gerald. But aloud she only said:

"Thank you so much for being so kind to me."

"Was I?" The smile deepened into something like lazy amusement. "It must have been an oversight. It isn't in my nature really." And with a slight nod to her, he turned away into the dusk again.

As Valerie went slowly through the darkened garden, she thought:

"He didn't tell me his name. I suppose he was motoring through and is staying only one night in the village.

But he knew the name of Monks Alder. Yet I don't think I mentioned it. I suppose Mrs. Thomas at the Crown told him. She usually says all she knows about people, and quite a lot she doesn't."

The next morning she woke with that reluctance which always means that a sense of disaster lingers in the back of the mind.

For a moment she lay there watching the sunlight on the wall, and the slender moving shadow of a sprig of honeysuckle that was tap-tapping on the window pane.

It was a heavenly day, the sun was shining, she was in her own dear room at Monks Alder, yet –

And then she remembered with dreadful clearness. It was no longer her room really. She had to make plans about leaving, and there was no one – not even Larry – who cared very much about her going.

The remembrance of Larry's part in this tragedy brought a sharper pain with it this morning. Last night she had been stunned by the surprise and, to tell the truth, sustained by her own anger. Now she was more inclined to grieve for the Larry who had been, rather than despise the Larry who had failed her last night.

It seemed much easier in the morning light to make excuses for him – to remember the special difficulties of his position – and to wonder if she had been hasty and unjust.

But there was no way back now. She reminded herself ruthlessly that, in the end, he *had* let her go, rather than have trouble with his mother. His mother who was petty enough to believe that the description "orphan" really altered one for the worse.

For the first time Valerie wondered if she were an inferior person because of it. No breath of snobbery had ever touched a thing which Aunt Evelyn did or said, and the problem had never presented itself to Valerie before. Now it somehow made her feel miserable and uncertain of herself.

Presently Mabel, the elderly housekeeper, brought in her breakfast, because, by doctor's orders, she still had breakfast in bed.

She got up as soon as she had eaten it, but was immediately frustrated in any plans for anything but rest by Mabel shepherding her into the garden, installing her in a cane chair, and supplying her with a newspaper.

Ten minutes later Mabel appeared again, holding a couple of letters which she was examining with frank thoroughness.

"Here's the post. Nothing for you. Only two letters for Him. One's got a London postmark. I wonder what that is? Business, I suppose. That means more money for him, I'll be bound. Business always means money for that sort."

Valerie tactfully refrained from comment and, after ascertaining that the second letter had an indecipherable postmark and was addressed in handwriting which might be a woman's "though of course it *could* be a man's," Mabel went indoors again.

She brought Valerie her lunch out of doors, arranging it with the care and attention which she never grudged to the people of whom she approved.

"That Mr. Ward rang up," she informed Valerie then. "Wanted to see Them urgently. I wonder why."

"Didn't he say what he wanted?" Valerie looked interested.

"No, miss. I told him They wouldn't be in till this afternoon, and he said he'd come round then. Not that *I* want to see him round here," Mabel added. She disapproved of the solicitor who had dealt with Aunt Evelyn's estate, never quite clearing him of blame in her own mind for not contriving to see that Miss Valerie "got *some*thing."

Valerie stayed out in the garden until she heard the car returning late in the afternoon. Then she went indoors reluctantly, to find both of them in the lounge, and both looking rather expectant as she came in.

Perhaps even they felt that yesterday's interview had ended on an unfortunate note, because Susan said, "Hello, Val," in a faintly placatory way, and Gerald said, "Had a good day in the garden?"

Valerie answered them both absently, and then went straight to the point.

"I'm afraid it will be rather a shock for you, but Larry and I have broken off our engagement."

"Wh – what?" stammered Susan dismayedly, while Gerald said:

"Broken it off? What on earth is the fellow thinking about?"

Valerie felt it was beyond her to interpret Larry's thoughts for Gerald, so she simply said, with as little expression as possible:

"I am sure you won't expect me to go into the reasons. The point is that it's quite final, and now I must stand on my own feet."

Gerald's face darkened at once.

"Look here, Val – this doesn't alter our position. My mother and sisters –"

"Yes, I know." Valerie cut across quite coolly. "Obviously I shall have to get a job of some sort and –"

"That's the idea!" Gerald interrupted in his turn. "Just the thing to take you out of yourself."

"Yes, I daresay. But just at the moment, there, there's some difficulty. Dr. Anderton says that I – I can't possibly do any work for" – at the expressions on the faces of her hearers, she nervously halved the minimum period – "for three months, and –"

"Oh, nonsense, Valerie!" Gerald was emphatic. "He's just fussing. I know these country doctors. Never seen you look better myself, except that you're a bit weak."

Valerie thought she must surely be more than "a bit" weak, because as Gerald ran on, justifying the idea of her taking up work at once, she found that ridiculous desire to cry unrestrainedly coming over her again. By keeping quite quiet and biting her lip hard, she managed to conquer the impulse.

Gerald was already talking brightly about her "going up to London and having a look round."

"And after all, Val, we don't want to be ungenerous about things. You must let me give you fifty quid to get along with while you're looking for a job. A gift, you know – not a loan. A girl can live carefully on that for two or three weeks." (He appeared to think she would walk to London since there was no mention of fare.) "You've got some beautiful clothes your aunt brought you. You won't need anything for a long while. Why, you'll manage splendidly!"

"It's very – kind of you, Gerald." Valerie bit her lip again, almost physically incapable of voicing another appeal. But the overwhelming sense of her broken health forced her to say something. "Could you possibly put up with me here for a month longer, just until I'm a little stronger? I don't mind turning out of my room, if you want it for your mother. I could – I could have the little room next to Mabel's –" The desire to cry stopped her from saying more. But she had already said too much.

"I'm sorry, Val." Gerald's mouth had become warningly thin again. "You're just imagining things about your health – indulging yourself, and –"

"Mr. Ward to see you," announced Mabel in a tone which implied that she could not imagine why anyone wanted to see Gerald and Susan.

Valerie would willingly have made her escape at this point, but Mr. Ward paused so long in the doorway while the opening civilities were exchanged that, by the time traffic was flowing normally again, it was impossible to withdraw without discourtesy.

She went over to the window instead, and stared out into the garden, the bright colours of the flowers blurring and mingling rather mistily as she blinked back tears from her eyes.

She heard Mr. Ward speaking about "a most extraordinary circumstance," but her attention was not arrested until the astounding words:

"At no time did any of us suppose that Mrs Hanson had any children."

Valerie swung round, to see expressions of almost ludicrous dismay freezing on the faces of Susan and Gerald.

"She *had* none!" Susan's tone implied that it was an impropriety beyond even the limits of Aunt Evelyn.

"Unfortunately – as one might say" – Mr. Ward

coughed – "it seems that she had. Perhaps I might ask Miss Eaton if she had any idea of this?" He turned to Valerie.

But Valerie looked as bewildered as anyone else.

"That Aunt Evelyn had a family? I don't think that can be right. She never spoke of any and –"

"Not a family exactly," Mr. Ward explained accurately. "One son. A young man of nearly thirty now."

"But Aunt Evelyn was only forty-eight when she died." Susan was nearly in tears.

"Ridiculous!" Gerald found his voice at last. "The fellow's an impostor. No question about it."

"My dear sir, there *is* no question about it, as you say." Mr. Ward was exceedingly ruffled that anyone should doubt credentials which he himself had accepted. "We advertised in the usual way, of course, for anyone making a claim against the estate. It seems Mrs. Hanson's son saw the notice and, very properly, applied to me in person."

"It *isn't* her son," reiterated poor Susan in a voice that rose to a sharp squeak at the end of the sentence.

Mr. Ward – who thought little of women in any case – gave her a glance of hardly veiled scorn.

"I know Aunt Evelyn was married very young," Valerie said doubtfully. "And I always understood that her husband died many years ago – in Canada, I think."

"Quite true." Mr. Ward corroborated the last part of this rather graciously. "He died in Canada. But not more than five or ten years ago. What happened was that Mrs. Hanson and her husband *separated* half a dozen years after their marriage."

"And are you suggesting that the husband took a

young child with him to Canada? It's –"

"I am not *suggesting* anything," snapped the lawyer. "I am telling you the facts as they have been told to me."

Gerald drew out his handkerchief slowly and wiped his forehead. But it was Susan who took up the fight then.

"Everyone knows that it's always from Canada or Australia that bogus relations appear."

A bleak smile flickered over Mr. Ward's face.

"We are dealing with fact just now," he pointed out politely, "not romantic fiction. It seems that Mrs. Hanson was on the stage in her younger days, and that, against her husband's wishes, she continued to after her marriage."

"She must have started as a pa – pantomime fairy, if your dates are right," put in Susan, who really was in tears by now.

"I couldn't tell you about that, I'm sure," retorted Mr. Ward coldly. "She had her – admirers, and her husband seems to have been jealous – with or without reason."

Valerie had an angry impulse to state that it must certainly have been without, but – suddenly remembering a special way Aunt Evelyn could smile when she wanted her own way – she remained silent and let Mr. Ward go on with his story.

"One admirer seems to have – er – caused more trouble than the others – again I cannot say whether with reason or not. These things are, after all, very much a matter of hearsay now. But when the young man was killed, as he was, in a plane crash it was found that he had left the whole of his fortune to Mrs. Hanson."

"So *that's* where it all came from!" exclaimed Gerald

bitterly, as though one might have expected something to go wrong with it in those circumstances.

"Mr. Hanson took this as conclusive evidence that he had been – er – justified in his suspicions, and, possibly also dismayed by the idea that his wife was now much richer than he could hope to be, he took the child and went to Canada, where he started life again and never communicated with her."

"Fantastic!" Gerald snorted. "Anyone can tell a cock-and-bull story like that."

"Marriage and birth certificates are, however, rather difficult to forge," pointed out Mr. Ward dryly. "In this country," he added, taking no responsibility for what happened in less enlightened countries.

Valerie nodded thoughtfully. Then she looked up with sudden light breaking on her.

"*That* was why Aunt Evelyn never made a will. I always thought it was strangely unlike her to be so – so unbusinesslike. She could never quite make up her mind to will her money to someone else, in case one day her own son turned up."

"Perhaps." Mr. Ward was not prepared to give an enthusiastic welcome to any theory he had not formed himself. "Anyway, he has turned up now. He has apparently done very well and is now an executive with a big international oil company. He is in England on a business trip."

"And where," inquired Gerald coldly, "is this – this very doubtful claimant?"

"Well, I think, from the sounds, that he is in your hall at the moment," remarked Mr. Ward, not without a certain dry pleasure. "He sent me on ahead to prepare you, and said he would call on his – ah – relations later this afternoon."

"Here's a gentleman who says he's Mr. Hanson," announced Mabel in a somewhat unorthodox manner.

And into the room – once more with that imperturbable smile – walked the man who had carried Valerie home the previous evening.

CHAPTER III

VALERIE'S first reaction to this somewhat melodramatic entry was a great desire to laugh.

Mr. Ward, she could not help thinking, looked as pleased as a conjuror who had just produced a rabbit from a hat, Gerald as bewildered as if his hat had been used for the purpose, and Susan as dismayed as if the rabbit had turned into a boa-constrictor.

The newcomer, on the other hand, appeared to share her own amusement, though his, "How do you do, Cousin Susan?" was a miracle of composure. Susan stammered out some conventional reply, but Gerald achieved nothing more than a slight and very stiff bow.

Unabashed, their visitor completed his greetings by shaking hands with Valerie, and then remarked to Susan and Gerald:

"I'm afraid you must be pretty sick to see me, as a matter of fact."

This might be the absolute and literal truth, but it was indecent to say so, and the expressions of Susan and her husband indicated as much.

"Surprised would perhaps describe it better," Gerald said coldly.

"I have explained everything to Mr. and Mrs. Manders," observed Mr. Ward firmly at this point, in case it should be supposed that he was responsible for the surprise.

"But we naturally feel that some considerable proof of this – this most extraordinary claim is called for," Gerald added heavily.

"Naturally," agreed the claimant cheerfully. "I am sure Mr. Ward is prepared to show you all the papers necessary to establish my claim, and, of course, I am perfectly willing to answer any inquiries you care to make. Unknown relatives can't expect to turn up at a moment's notice and be acclaimed with enthusiasm."

"No," Susan agreed plaintively. "We had accepted the fact that everything – that everything belonged to *us*."

"To your cousin and you?" Their preposterous visitor indicated Valerie with a slight gesture.

"*Val*? Certainly *not*." Here at least Susan's irritation could have full play. "Valerie is no relation at all." She looked at Valerie as though she had no real right to be there.

"But you must have seemed like relations?" The suggestion was perfectly smooth. "Valerie had lived here for many years, I thought."

"Yes, but that isn't the same thing at all," Susan protested fretfully, adding, without much point, that "blood was thicker than water."

Valerie was unable to tell from their visitor's expression whether he too subscribed to this favourite view of Susan's. After all, she supposed a little wearily, he was probably no more anxious than Susan or Gerald to encourage a penniless hanger-on. She felt miserable and uncomfortable to remember now how frank she had been to him, the previous evening, about her exact position.

"Of course I had no idea who you were yesterday

evening," she said softly and a little shyly.

"Of course not."

But, quiet though the words were, Gerald heard them and swung round on her.

"So you've been talking to him?" he exclaimed angrily, as though she might have given away some vital information.

"Of course she talked to me. A charming and sociable girl, your cousin." Again that lazy but slightly dangerous smile. "I met her near the house yesterday evening and we – passed the time of day."

"Haven't you done enough mischief without tattling about things that don't concern you?" snapped Gerald, rounding on Valerie. He, like Susan, felt that here was someone at least on whom he could safely vent his irritation and disappointment. "First you worm your way into a family where you don't belong, then you smash up your benefactor in a motor accident, then –"

Valerie was never quite sure what happened next. But a moment later Gerald was lying flat on his back on what – for two happy months – he had imagined to be his own hearthrug. Susan uttered a little squeak of fright while Mr. Ward clucked protestingly. He was not used to having even the most disagreeable of his clients dealt with in this manner.

White with rage, and a certain amount of shock, Gerald began to get to his feet again.

"I don't know what you think you're doing, Mr – Mr. –"

"Hanson is my name. Nigel Hanson."

"You can't come here with your roughneck ways. Hitting a man in his own house –"

51

"Mine, I think," Nigel Hanson said with a smile. "And if you don't like my ways, you know what to do about it."

"Gentlemen, gentlemen," protested Mr. Ward, but he only received a very sour look from Gerald, who greatly resented the implication that he was at all responsible for this undignified scene. To tell the truth, no one could have wished for it less than he had.

"Perhaps you had better apologise to the lady." Nigel Hanson showed no sign of having lost his good temper throughout this little scene.

"Apologise?" repeated Gerald incredulously. "To *Valerie*?"

"To Valerie," agreed Nigel Hanson pleasantly.

Gerald could hardly hide his chagrined astonishment at such a notion. But when, either by accident or design, his visitor thoughtfully passed his left hand backwards and forwards over the knuckles of his right, Gerald turned to Valerie and said sulkily:

"Sorry, Val. Spoke a bit hastily, I'm afraid. No harm meant."

Valerie, almost as embarrassed and surprised as he that an apology should actually be offered, assured him hastily that it was all right. She secretly thought that Nigel Hanson was extracting just a trifle too much amusement from this scene of cousinly reconciliation. But she could not help enjoying the novelty of having Gerald forced to treat her like a human being again.

Conversation, which might well have languished at this point, was galvanised into uneasy life once more by Nigel's suggesting that Gerald and Susan should inspect the proofs of his claim, which Mr. Ward had brought with him. A visit to the dentist would hardly have given them less pleasure, but the matter was not one which could be shelved, and Gerald at least made a sign of sulky acquiescence.

"I don't expect you will want me around," Nigel added with a slightly too sympathetic air of tact. "So embarrassing to have to ask suspicious questions in front of the suspect, isn't it? Perhaps" – he turned to Valerie – "perhaps Valerie would show me the garden. I'm sure she knows it better than anyone else here."

Amused though she was, Valerie felt this was unnecessary cruelty to her cousins. But when Gerald snapped, "It might be as well," she saw that his one idea was to get this appalling newcomer out of the way while he did all he could to find some weakness in the claim.

Valerie opened the french window, and said a little shyly, "We'll go this way, shall we?"

As he followed her into the garden Nigel Hanson had all the air of intending to ask correct questions about flowers and plants, but as soon as they moved out of earshot of the others, what he said was:

"Why don't you like to see people taking some of their own medicine?"

Valerie laughed, rather nervously. She was not entirely at ease with this stranger – partly because of her candour to him on the previous evening, but mostly because she thought that caustic sense of humour might turn in some new direction without warning.

"Well, I – suppose I can't help knowing just how horrified and bewildered Susan and Gerald are feeling at this moment."

"Which ought to afford you a great deal of innocent

pleasure, my charming adopted sister."

Valerie gave him a startled glance.

"I don't feel at all like your adopted sister," she said rather hastily.

"No," he agreed, "I can't say that my feelings towards you are exactly brotherly." And the way he said that, with his lazy smile directed full on her, made Valerie flush unexpectedly.

"Is this – is this your usual opening?" she inquired a trifle dryly.

"Meaning?"

"Are you in the habit of going about knocking down the people you don't like and being – devastatingly frank to the others?"

"Impossible behaviour on the part of the new heir, you mean?"

"No – no. Unconventional, shall we say?"

"It's a method which saves a great deal of time and trouble," he assured her carelessly.

"What? – knocking people down?"

He laughed then, and very lightly took her arm.

"Confess – you were just as pleased as I was to see Cousin Gerald lying on his back."

Valerie laughed reluctantly, though she refused to answer that directly. After a moment she asked curiously:

"What are you going to do about things? I mean – so far as Susan and Gerald are concerned."

"As soon as they have been reluctantly convinced of my genuine identity I shall ask them to get out."

"Just like that? – quite brutally?"

"As brutally as I can," he agreed cheerfully. "I told

54

you – *I* do like seeing people take their own medicine, even if you don't."

"It doesn't strike you that you are being just as – as unkind as they are?"

"Of course it does. That's what I intend. It's the only thing they understand."

Her faintly troubled air seemed to amuse him, and, glancing at her, he said:

"You're much too tender-hearted, Valerie."

"No, I'm not really. I can think the harshest things of them both without much difficulty. But I can't help knowing they must be appallingly disappointed."

"Do them good," was the callous rejoinder. "Shall we sit down here?" He paused by the group of chairs under the trees, where Valerie had spent her morning.

"I thought you wanted to see the garden." She smiled without looking at him. "Are you tired already?"

"No," he said. "But I think you are."

Valerie glanced at him curiously again. She wondered very much what to make of him. One moment he was full of a sort of cheerful callousness, the next he was remembering to look after a sick girl he had only just met.

She sat down, since he insisted, and he too slumped comfortably in a garden chair and looked round him with a great deal of satisfaction.

"This," he remarked conversationally, "is what I always thought England ought to be."

Valerie smiled.

"It's quite typical of a certain part of England," she told him. "So you spent nearly all your life in Canada?"

"Yes."

55

"Perhaps that –"

"– explains a lot?" he suggested.

"I didn't say that." Valerie flushed.

"But thought it very politely to yourself," he said, without rancour.

"No, I didn't. I'm not quite used to your ways – that's all. But then I daresay you're not used to mine. For all I know, you may be thinking me an impossible person in some way or another."

He smiled straight at her again in that slightly disconcerting manner.

"No, Valerie, I'm not thinking you impossible," was what he said. "Suppose we leave that word to describe Susan and Gerald, shall we?"

"Very well." Valerie leant back in her chair, feeling oddly at ease. "So you are really going to send them away?" she pressed him after a moment.

"Tomorrow, if I can."

"Tomorrow?" Valerie sat up quickly. "Then I think it's time I started to pack."

"I said 'them,' Valerie, not 'you'."

"Oh, but –" she paused confusedly.

"Yes?"

"If you expect them to leave your house at a moment's notice, you must feel even more strongly that it is time I went. They are at least your cousins."

He made a face.

"Must you really remind me of that? Besides, the objectionable Gerald is only a cousin by marriage. And as I should most certainly have forbidden the banns of that marriage if I had had anything to do with it, I hardly see why I need be made to pay exaggerated attention to the relationship."

Valerie smiled faintly.

"Very well, argue it that way if you like. But with me there isn't even that shadowy relationship to bother about."

"Good heavens, Valerie!" he said. "What a value you set on mere relationship. I'm astonished and faintly disappointed in you."

Valerie's smile was just a little sad then, and she said rather softly:

"I've been made to do so in the last few weeks."

She was looking away from him as she said that, and she didn't see the way those very light, cynical eyes softened.

"I suppose," he said slowly, "that my mother brought you to this house because she liked you, and kept you here for twelve years because she loved you. I find that something much more real and important than a mere cousinship. And I think, Valerie, that you agree with me."

"Oh" – she gave an unsteady little laugh, and on sudden impulse held out her hand to him. "That's terribly sweet of you. Much the nicest thing that has been said to me for a very long time. It wasn't only that she – that she loved me, you know." She looked down at the strong brown fingers that were holding her own. "I loved her too – so very much. To be sent away from here almost in disgrace – the way Susan and Gerald wanted it – was like being told that I had never deserved all her affection. That I just hadn't proved worthy of it."

"I know, I know." He looked down a little wonderingly at the hand he had taken, as though he too found a curious contrast between his own strong fingers and her rather delicate ones. "But it wasn't like that at all. Don't pay Gerald's mean little ideas the compliment of receiving so much attention."

"I won't," Valerie said slowly – and then wondered if she had somehow given the impression that she believed her dismissal from Monks Alder to have been postponed indefinitely.

"Of course I didn't mean that I – that I wasn't expecting to leave here anyway, but –"

"We'll talk about that later, Val. I think I see Mr. Ward making signs of distress or triumph from the window. Perhaps we ought to go back now and hear the result of the discussion."

"You go," Valerie said nervously. "They hate having me there, because they don't feel I have any real part in it."

"As you like." He looked amused again. "I'll come back and report later. But if you see me flung out on my back you'll know that my claim couldn't stand up to Gerald's investigation."

He crossed the lawn to the house once more, with that easy, almost careless, stride, and Valerie's gaze followed him very thoughtfully.

He really was rather an extraordinary person but, in an odd way, he *had* something of Aunt Evelyn about him. Not so much in appearance as in his uncompromising manner, and his disregard for what people might think. Aunt Evelyn had never allowed that there were things "one just didn't do" simply because other people didn't do them. If her own conscience and inclination indicated that they *should* be done – she did them.

And Aunt Evelyn, who had never liked Gerald, would certainly have enjoyed her son's method of dealing with him. Quite a number of people, reflected Valerie with a smile, must have *wanted* to knock Gerald down at one time or another. Nigel, it seemed, saw no reason why that desire should not be translated into action.

That, too, was like Aunt Evelyn. And it was also like her that he had selected as the offence to be dealt with, not any insult or slight to himself, but an unprovoked attack on someone unable to defend herself. There was something nice, and somehow reassuring, about that.

Presently, Valerie's curiosity getting the better of her nervousness, she strolled back across the lawn to the house again. But, when she came into the lounge, it was to find that Susan and Gerald had withdrawn from the field, and only Nigel and Mr. Ward remained – deep in conversation.

Nigel looked up, to remark with slightly indecent relish:

"They've retired to count their losses."

Mr. Ward frowned, cleared his throat, and conveyed his information in more conventional wording.

"I couldn't say for certain whether Mr. and Mrs. Manders have any intention of disputing Mr. Hanson's claim, but I think they realise that the evidence of identity is beyond question."

"Oh, I'm very gl –" Valerie hesitated, felt that the wording he had been going to use was hardly tactful, and changed her remark to, "I must congratulate you, Mr. Hanson."

59

Nigel said gravely:

"Let me congratulate *you*. Charming Cousin Susan and Gerald, I understand, are leaving tomorrow. That will make Monks Alder a whole lot more attractive, won't it?"

Valerie felt Mr. Ward's curious glance on her, and was annoyed to realise that she was flushing. He was wondering, of course, just what *she* was going to do. With the installing of the new bachelor owner, her departure became even more certain and necessary.

One of those horrible waves of panic, to which she was becoming all too used, assailed her again. Even Gerald's fifty pounds would certainly vanish in the present circumstances. And, although the amused championship of Nigel Hanson was acceptable, it did nothing towards solving her now most pressing problem.

He had said they would discuss her departure later, but since he was certainly a person who liked to do things quickly, he would want to install himself at Monks Alder without delay. And even anyone so unconventional as he must see that the pleasant little fiction of their being in some sense related would not cover the idea of her staying in the house one night after he entered into possssion of it.

Arden was not a village to allow that sort of thing to pass without copious – and highly scandalous – comment.

Evidently some such thoughts were occupying Mr. Ward's mind as he gazed speculatively at Valerie. And since she didn't know the answers to any of the all-too-obvious questions, she felt the flush grow even a little deeper.

It was Nigel who spoke first, breaking the slight, uneasy silence which had fallen.

"You won't be nervous alone here in the house, will you, Valerie?"

"No, I – I'm not at all nervous, of course," Valerie stammered slightly with relief and a queer emotion she could hardly put a name to. "And anyway, Mabel will be here with me – for the short time I shall be here," she added hastily.

He nodded non-committally, and simply said:

"Do you want any moral support when Susan and Gerald take their departure?"

That made Valerie smile a little, but she shook her head.

"All right. Then I can't say I'm so fond of their company that I want to see them again. I'll come over tomorrow evening, if I may, and see you when they have gone."

"Why, of course you may." She was faintly confused at the idea of having to give him permission to enter his own house. But he seemed to see nothing incongruous in it, and a few minutes later both he and Mr. Ward took their leave.

To Valerie, the rest of that day and the following morning had something of the character of a stage farce.

It was hard to believe that Susan – and, still more, Gerald – could have been so completely discomfited. They still breathed doubts and threats against the invader, and Gerald talked a great deal about "seeing his own solicitors the moment he got back to town," but it was obvious that all confidence in their own claims had really vanished.

Perhaps the most disconcerting – though amusing – part of all was that Nigel's unusual championship of Valerie seemed capable of extending quite a powerful protection to her even in his absence. Gerald made none of his customary attempts to bully her or work off his own chagrin on her. He asked almost respectfully about her first meeting with Nigel, and when he learnt that she had not even known who the newcomer was, he shook his head with a sigh and remarked that "it was a sad day for all of them," apparently under the impression that Valerie also was very much a loser by reason of the new heir's arrival.

"I don't know what he thinks I've lost," reflected Valerie amusedly. "But I suppose it is very gracious of him to allow me to share the same cloud of disaster as himself and Susan."

She was not going to be permitted to share anything more tangible, however. Any inquiries he made about her own future were tempered by very clear indications that she could not hope for help or shelter from them.

"Afraid we shan't be able to do much for you now, Valerie," was how Gerald put it, as though the withdrawal of the much grudged fifty pounds must represent a descent from wealth to penury. "If we'd been staying on here – Well, there it is. We're not. So I'm sure you'll understand –"

Valerie said that she understood.

He seemed astonished and annoyed that she was not leaving Monks Alder at least on the same day as Susan and himself, and her vague admission that she would be "leaving in a day or two," made him raise his eyebrows superciliously.

Afterwards Valerie overheard him remark to Susan:

"That cousin of yours has no pride. Now I suppose she's going to cadge from that swine. Well, she'll soon get herself talked about – hanging on at Monks Alder with an extremely questionable young man about."

She felt furious and miserable, and she longed to be able to say something crushing about her future plans. But there was nothing to say. Never before had she realised the power of money so acutely – or rather, the helplessness which went with the lack of it. If only she had been well enough to work! It was so ridiculous – so humiliating that at this very moment when she most needed to stand on her own feet, she was subject to these absurd fits of weakness and illness.

Surely one could *will* oneself to be stronger, thought Valerie angrily. But she found one could do nothing of the sort, and so one had to accept the incredible situation that one's future was more or less dependent on the whim of some man who had been a stranger forty-eight hours ago.

When Susan and Gerald had finally departed, Mabel remarked, "Good riddance to bad rubbish," with a relish which showed that she thought Fate was behaving properly at last.

"And now, Valerie," she added, "don't you fret about that lost engagement ring. There's as good fish in the sea as ever came out of it. And I've just been thinking what a fine thing it would be if this new young man was to marry you. Then you and me wouldn't have to leave Monks Alder at all."

Valerie smiled.

"The chief objection being, Mabel, that we might detest each other inside a week. Two days is rather a short time to tell, you know."

"Queerer things have happened," Mabel retorted. "You only have to watch the telly to see *that*."

But even this corroborative evidence failed to shake Valerie, and she was smiling still as she went off into the garden, to sit under the trees and enjoy to the full the luxury of a place free once more of Susan and Gerald.

She supposed Nigel Hanson would soon be putting in an appearance, and she was aware of a half-nervous, half-pleasurable sense of anticipation as she waited for him.

When he did come she felt her heart lift.

"Why, Nigel –" she began, and then stopped.

"Why, Valerie," he said teasingly, and stood smiling down at her, that lazy air less in evidence now, and a singularly authoritative touch about his manner. "So they've gone?"

"Yes, they've gone. Mabel says 'good riddance to bad rubbish.'"

"I endorse Mabel's judgment." He sat down in the chair opposite Valerie and, stretching out his long legs, looked very much at ease.

He smiled at her and leant forward suddenly, those half cynical, half friendly eyes fixed on her. "I came here this afternoon to ask you something, and because the time's short and life's going at a terrific pace just now, I have to be in a crazy hurry too. It has to be this way or not at all. Val, will you marry me?"

Valerie swallowed in sheer astonishment.

"But you don't know the first thing about me!"

"Oh yes. The first thing – and that's about all. It's all

you know of me too. But that isn't really the point. I want you to go on living here at Monks Alder, Valerie, but, you see, I want to know it and enjoy it too while I'm over here. And in due course, I intend the place to go to you."

He was watching her with a curious intensity as he spoke. It made her realise that, even if the scene were fantastic, at least it was deadly serious.

"But, even if you want to be so extravagantly, unbelievably generous as to – leave me Monks Alder eventually, why do you think you have to marry me in order to do it?" she said gently. "There's no need for you to have me here. I'll leave tomorrow – tonight, if you like, since the time is so short. Then you –"

"And where," he asked quietly, "would you go?"

"Oh, I – well, I – There would be somewhere, Nigel. It's ridiculous to think of a man marrying me just to give me a home."

"Marriages have been arranged for less," he reminded her with a smile. "But that isn't the beginning and end of it. Don't imagine I am working up some sort of quixotic offer because I'm sorry for you. I want you to be here – as well as Monks Alder. You are part of it. The best part, I'm inclined to think. Anyway, forget everything I said except one thing. Will you marry me, Val?"

CHAPTER IV

EVEN when he had repeated his question, Valerie found herself still groping for an answer. One could not go on staring at him in silence, and yet – what *did* one say when, in all seriousness, one was offered a fantastic solution to a pressing problem?

When words finally came, they avoided the real issue, of course, for it was impossible to say "yes" or "no" in cold blood at this point.

"Aren't you being a bit too impulsive, even for you?" was what she said – gently, as though she were speaking to someone younger than herself. "One can't take on anything so serious as – marriage without a good reason."

"There is a good reason. There are several good reasons."

She regarded him in perplexed silence, and he said quietly:

"Val, what had you planned to do?"

"Before you suggested this, you mean? Nothing. That's just the trouble. Absolutely nothing. And now if I should accept – what you suggest, it would simply be like grabbing at the chance of a house and home at all costs."

"Not to me," he countered quickly. "That's not how it would seem to me."

"No?" The slight lift of her eyebrows was humorous

and characteristic. "Well, that's exactly how it seems to me, Nigel. I should despise myself for it always. And after a while you would come to despise me too."

"Oh no, it isn't like that at all. *You* aren't doing all the taking. Listen, Val –" He sat down on the grass at her feet, not looking at her, but away from her, his light hazel eyes slightly narrowed as though he were concentrating on finding exactly the right words. "I've had a good many experiences in my life – good, bad, indifferent – odd things and ordinary things, a certain amount of tragedy and a certain amount of comedy. But I know that in all of that I've missed the most exciting – I suppose the most mysterious – experience of all. I've never known a woman really well. I don't mean just that I've never had a love affair. Women haven't had any place in my life."

She glanced down at him, conscious of an odd desire to touch the dark head that was rather close to her knee. But he didn't notice the change in her expression, and he went on very earnestly.

"I can't even remember my mother, of course, and my childhood was made up of spells at boarding-school and holidays with my father. He was wonderfully good to me – don't think anything else – but he was a peculiar chap and always fought shy of women as though they were the devil. I never felt the lack of something I hadn't known – at least, not as a kid, and not when I first started out on my own, very thrilled and pleased with myself that I was a man and doing a man's job at last. But lately –" His voice trailed away and his gaze became even more thoughtful. The silence lasted so long that at last she prompted him gently.

"Lately, Nigel?"

"Eh?" He twisted round suddenly with a smile and rested his arm lightly on her knee. "Lately I've known that somehow I've missed a good deal somewhere. I was more than ever aware of it when I – found you in the wood that evening, and most of all when I first saw you here on this lawn. Don't think I'm fanciful, and don't think I'm making it all up to suit your circumstances. I want more than anything else in the world to be able to come back sometimes to you and Monks Alder, and to know that you both mean home."

Valerie bit her lip. She was strangely touched – perhaps because every word he said bore the stamp of absolute sincerity.

A little shyly she put out her hand, and that time she did touch his hair.

"You don't look much into the future, Nigel, do you? You're not – afraid of the future?"

"No, not at all." He was very still as her hand touched him, rather as though he thought that any movement of his might frighten her. His voice was unusually gentle too as he added, "And if you will let me look after your future, you shall have nothing to fear either. What do you say?"

"That I suppose no tiresomely penniless and half-invalid girl has ever received a more generous offer," Valerie replied slowly. "I thought at first it would be crazy to accept. Now – I think – perhaps it would be crazy to refuse."

He had flushed at her first sentence. But now he actually paled unexpectedly.

"You mean you will marry me?"

"Yes, I will marry you, if –"

"There *are* no 'ifs,'" he told her quickly. And then, with odd, but rather charming, formality – "Thank you, Val."

Valerie laughed then – a little laugh of genuine amusement.

He glanced at her with slightly raised eyebrows though without resentment.

"And the joke about that is –"

"That *you* should thank *me,* of course. It's a funny idea that you should offer me the earth, so to speak, and then thank me for accepting it."

He smiled, but rather seriously.

"Perhaps," he said, "I feel that what I'm getting in return is worth at least as much as I'm offering."

She wanted rather to ask him what he meant by that – just what he supposed he was getting "in return." But she hardly saw how she could word the question. This was not like accepting a job. You couldn't ask bluntly what the terms were. You took the plunge – a little breathlessly – and what came afterwards remained a matter of conjecture.

One thing was reassuring. He made no attempt to kiss her or to offer the endearments which one associated with an engagement. Why, when Larry and she –

Rather frightenedly Valerie dragged back her thoughts. What had happened between Larry and herself mattered not at all now. The two cases could hardly have been more different, and the less she thought about that other time the better.

"I suppose," she said slowly, "that we had better do it as soon as possible. One – I mean, *we* – could be married in a day or two by special licence, couldn't we?"

"We could." He was smiling at her. "I've forgotten the exact number of hours' or days' notice one has to give. Only people who make a habit of marriage ever really know these details, I imagine. But if we said" – he glanced at her – "Monday, I think we should cover it."

"Monday – that's three days from now."

"Yes. Long enough?"

"I think so."

"Long enough to get your trousseau and not long enough to change your mind, eh?"

"I shan't get a trousseau," Valerie told him. "And I shan't change my mind."

He laughed, but it was a pleased – almost a relieved – laugh, as if even he had not really dared to suppose that everything would turn out so exactly as he wanted it.

Only when he was going did he even attempt to touch her, and then it was no more than to take her arm lightly as she strolled with him to the gate.

"I ought to make earnest protestations, Val, about promising to be a good husband to you and all that."

"But it wouldn't be very appropriate, would it?"

"The devil! Wouldn't it? Don't you expect me to be a good husband, then?"

She laughed.

"Oh, I didn't mean that. I meant –"

"Yes?"

"Well, it isn't really much like the usual marriage, is it? I mean – you probably won't feel very much like my husband or – or I feel very much like your wife."

They paused by the gate just then, and he looked at her rather curiously through the gathering dusk.

"Think not?" And, bending his head, he kissed her full on the lips. Not aggressively, not even possessively, but as though he had every right to do it. "Good-night, Val."

"Good-night, Nigel." She was more than a little disturbed by that kiss. But he had turned away immediately and there was no chance to say anything – even if she had felt like saying it.

Very thoughtfully she went back into the house – where the expectant glances of Mabel prompted her to say with devastating nonchalance:

"Oh, Mabel, I'm going to marry Mr. Hanson."

Mabel, however, seemed to regard the arrangement as providential rather than peculiar.

"There now," she exclaimed with real feeling, "isn't love a wonderful thing! Here are you and me settled for life, and no thanks to that good-for-nothing young Larry Bowdon either."

Valerie agreed hastily that love was indeed wonderful, but hurried the conversation a step further on. She had no wish to discuss Larry with Mabel. Indeed, she must try not even to think of Larry any more, because if she did she could not help remembering how often and how happily she had anticipated a future which centred round *him,* and not round the insistent and disturbing stranger who had suddenly taken over the management of her life.

"We're going to be married next week, Mabel. On Monday. It will be very quiet, of course."

"But, Valerie, you don't mean you're not going to be

married in white, with a veil and all? Oh, it doesn't seem decent somehow!"

"I'm afraid that's the way it will have to be." Valerie smiled at her. "I'll wear that flowered blue frock that Aunt Evelyn gave me. It – it was the last thing she gave me and – there was never a chance to wear it. That makes it nice, somehow – the fact that she gave it to me."

"Well, it's new anyway, and I suppose blue is the next best to white," Mabel grumbled. "But it won't be any good unless it's a very fine day, mind. One shower of rain and it'll be hanging round you. *I* know what happens with them frilly things once they get out in the rain."

"It isn't going to rain, Mabel," Valerie assured her. "Doesn't your romantic soul tell you that the sun must certainly shine for this – this unusual and delightful wedding?"

"Well, it is a nice romance and all," Mabel admitted. "It's sudden enough, in all conscience," she added, apparently of the opinion that romance was necessarily a sudden business.

Valerie thought more than once of Mabel's remark during that strange week-end. It *was* "sudden enough, in all conscience," and sometimes she wondered if it were really she – Valerie Eaton – who was embarking on this extraordinary adventure.

Once or twice she had moments of cold panic – worse even than when she had first realised that she was penniless and too ill to do anything about it. But she calmed herself determinedly – usually with the uanswerable question, "And what is the alternative?"

To many girls, she supposed, it would have seemed a heaven-sent opportunity. A good-looking, attractive husband suddenly appearing out of nowhere just in time to save her from goodness knew what sort of dilemma. Could one ask more?

Either from tact or from some other unexplained reason, Nigel made only brief visits to Monks Alder during that week-end. Perhaps he imagined Valerie had a good deal to occupy her time, or perhaps he just thought she would like that last day or two to herself, so that she could adjust her thoughts and feelings – and even change her mind if the prospect seemed too strange and terrifying after all.

But Valerie had no thought of changing her mind. She only wondered uneasily once or twice if she ought to let Larry know – and, if so, in just what way she could do so.

Then, before she had settled that point, the short time had slipped away. She was waking once more to the sunshine of her bedroom at Monks Alder as she had on a thousand other mornings, but today there was something different.

"This," said Valerie aloud, "is my wedding-day."

She thought it might make it all seem a little more real when she put it into words. But the situation remained as fantastic as when he had first made that proposal in the garden.

Feeling singularly calm in spite of everything, Valerie got up and dressed.

Nothing about this wedding of hers was arranged in quite what Mabel called "the right way." There were no bridesmaids, no guests, no one of Valerie's own family to give her away. Worst of all, in Mabel's eyes, Nigel himself was to come to take her to the church.

He was waiting for her in the drawing-room. He, too, had been standing by the window, but he turned at once when she came in.

He looked very tall as he came across the room to her, and his light-grey suit seemed to deepen the tan of his skin and bring out the vividness of his dark colouring. Only his eyes were light – with that curious brightness which made them so expressive and so vividly alive.

Taking both her hands, he smiled down at her, without attempting to kiss her.

"How sweet you look, Val."

"Do I?" She felt faintly shy suddenly. "Aunt Evelyn chose the dress. It was – the last thing she gave me."

"My mother chose your wedding-dress?" he repeated slowly. "Oh, there's something very nice about that, Val."

She thought so too. It was nice too – and very reassuring – to remember that this man *was* Aunt Evelyn's son. Somehow it made him less of a stranger and more like someone whom she could trust with the direction of her life.

"Are you ready?"

"Yes."

"Shall we go, then?"

She nodded.

As they crossed the lawn he said reflectively:

"It's rather odd to be walking to one's wedding."

"Yes. But Mabel says that everything about this wedding is odd."

Then Valerie felt she could hardly have put it more tactlessly, and she hastily added:

"No bridesmaids and – and that sort of thing, I mean. Nor anyone of the family to give me away."

"But you haven't got any family, have you?" He seemed amused rather than affronted. "Except Cousin Susan. And on that reckoning, Gerald would be the right person to give you away."

They both laughed at that, and Valerie said:

"Nigel, you have such a nice sense of humour."

"So have you, my dear. That's partly why I –"

"Why you what?"

To her surprise he looked very faintly put out.

"Nothing. I'll tell you another time."

There was no opportunity to press the point further, even if she had wanted to, because by now they were inside the cool shadow of the porch, and the church which Valerie had known since childhood stretched before them – quiet, sunlit, and most strangely empty. It seemed to her that only she and Nigel were there. Then she saw Mabel, beaming at her, and she was aware that there were a few other people after all – people from the village mostly, who made it their business to attend any wedding, christening or funeral, on the theory that it was always a pity to miss a free show.

She didn't remember very much of her wedding afterwards. Not that she was nervous – in fact, she was oddly calm and collected. But the whole ceremony had a touch of fantasy about it, as though it were the kind of scene one might dream on a sunny afternoon, and then wake to find that tea was ready, and one was not married to a stranger after all.

As soon as possible she and Nigel escaped from the congratulations and their expressions of surprise. Back home once more she was suddenly terribly afraid that Nigel would take her in his arms – make some demonstration of affection or be possessive with her. It was not that she wanted to be anything but fair – she was determined to play the game properly by him – but at the moment she was more nervous and strung up than she had realised, and she felt that if he kissed her now she would probably either push him away or burst into tears.

She was not put to any such test, however. He smilingly took her flowers from her and gave them to Mabel to put in water. Then he said:

"Come on, Val. Let's go out in the car, and not stop for lunch until we've got up an appetite after all this excitement. Don't bother to change. You look sweet as you are. Just slip on a coat while I go down to the village and get the car."

"No, wait. I'll come with you." She found his matter-of-fact manner oddly soothing. "I won't keep you a moment."

As she ran upstairs to fetch a coat, she thought:

"I don't feel different in any way – and it wasn't so nerve-racking after all. How I should like a long drive! It was clever of him to think of it."

Mabel waved to them benevolently as they went off, and called to them to "have a good time" as though they were a couple of children in her care.

"Let's go this way." Valerie instinctively turned off through the side gate, knowing that this would take them by quiet country lanes, and save them the ordeal of a walk through the main street of the village, where the news of their wedding had probably already penetrated, and where they would have to run the gauntlet of plenty of curious glances.

He must have sensed something of her feelings, because he remarked thoughtfully after a moment:

"I suppose there's a good deal of gossip in a place like this?"

"Oh yes," Valerie laughed. "Arden lives largely on gossip."

"And you will come in for plenty of it – charitable and otherwise?"

"I daresay." She shrugged. "I can bear it."

"Sure?" he smiled.

But she was not smiling any longer. Someone was coming towards them along the lane. Someone whose appearance held her gaze in fascinated dismay. He was the only person in sight except themselves, and in the narrow lane it would be impossible to do anything but stop and speak.

Of all the ways to meet Larry again, this was the most unfortunate!

Nigel didn't seem to notice her agitation. In fact, he noticed nothing until Larry came abreast of them – and stopped dead.

"Val! I – was just coming along to Monks Alder to see you. How are you?" The embarrassment – the candid touch of shame about him – tugged at Valerie's heart in a way that frightened her. How had she forgotten for a few days how dear and how boyish he was?

She tried frantically to put such thoughts away from her, and with an effort she steadied her voice.

77

"I'm all right, Larry. Quite all right, thank you." And then: "I should like you to meet Nigel. Nigel Hanson."

Larry accepted the introduction – politely but absently, as though his thoughts were certainly not on Valerie's companion. After the barest civilities, he turned to her again and said urgently:

"Val, I should like to speak with you alone for a few minutes. I'm sure Mr. Hanson will excuse us."

Nigel prepared to accept the dismissal gracefully, if a trifle mockingly. But Valerie, determined not to let things slide further, detained him as he was turning away by an agitated touch on his arm.

"No, there isn't anything private where – Nigel is concerned. You see – I ought to have explained before" – she faced Larry determinedly – "Nigel is – is my husband. We've just been married this morning."

It was not the way she would have chosen to tell Larry, for his sake even more than her own, but there was no choice now. She saw him whiten slowly, and his lips moved slightly, as though he were trying to voice some conventionality. Then, without a word, he turned on his heel and walked rapidly away without once looking back.

For a moment she stood there wordless, staring after him. It was Nigel's voice which finally recalled her to the present.

"That was the ex-fiancé, I take it?" He said that quite coolly, as though it all had very little to do with him.

"Yes." She could think of nothing to add to the one word.

"Hm. Tit for tat. I hope he feels punished for the way he treated you."

"Oh, don't talk like that!" She turned on him in sudden nervous anger. "Must you be cheaply cynical about everything?"

There was a rather dreadful little silence. Then he said:

"I'm sorry."

"No. I'm sorry, I had no right to say that, Nigel. Please forgive me."

"Don't be silly," he told her lightly. "There is nothing to forgive. People are never at their best on their wedding-day. I don't see why we should expect ourselves to be an exception."

"That's — generous of you," she said. But he only laughed and shrugged his shoulders.

They said very little more until they reached the inn where Nigel had garaged his car. But when Valerie was seated beside Nigel, and they were heading for the open country, she had a feeling of escape — as though they were running away, at least for the time, from a problem which had suddenly started to grow to unmanageable proportions.

"Do you know what I'd like to do, Nigel?"

"Well?" He smiled at the road ahead, without turning to look at her.

"I'd like us to go on driving all day — not to bother about the time we get home, but just to go on, stopping when were hungry and not planning anything definite all the day."

"It would be nice."

"Well — shall we do it? We can phone to Mabel from wherever we stop for lunch and tell her we shall not be in until late."

She wanted him to agree. She feverishly wanted to fill the day with new impressions, so that she could forget – or almost forget – that scene in the lane with Larry. But Nigel's enthusiastic consent was lacking.

"Sorry, Val dear, I'm afraid we can't."

"Afraid we can't?" She was already so curiously used to his indulgent air towards her that this first refusal to do what she wanted astonished her. "But don't you want to?"

"Nothing would please me better," he assured her with a smile. "But – I didn't tell you before, because I had an idea that we'd try to keep today unspoilt – I had a phone call first thing this morning. I have to go on an extended business tour of the Middle East, starting tomorrow. It means leaving tonight by the eight-thirty train."

"Leaving tonight!" Valerie repeated his words slowly. "Then you mean – you'll not have even *one* night at Monks Alder."

"No," he said, and his smile had a certain humorous significance. "I shall not have even one night at Monks Alder."

CHAPTER V

For several minutes there was silence between them – he apparently intent on his driving and she looking at the flying fields and hedges as though they engaged her deepest attention.

Then she spoke at last with a slight sigh.

"Nigel, I'm awfully sorry about it."

"Are you, Val?" His expression was slightly quizzical though he did not look at her. "That's very nice of you."

"Why 'nice'?" She spoke quickly.

"Because I believe you really mean what you say – you *are* sorry. And yet, from the sheerly selfish point of view, you ought to regard this as much the best and most comfortable solution for you."

"I wasn't thinking about that," she said rather soberly. "I was thinking that it's very hard on you not to have had any time at Monks Alder at all. And if it hadn't been for me, you would have."

He laughed.

"If it hadn't been for you, I probably should not have been there at all."

She looked astonished.

"Oh, but why, Nigel? What do you mean?"

"Eh?" He seemed to recollect himself. "I mean that I should probably have sold the place."

"*Sold* it? I thought you liked it so much!"

"I do. But it's no place for a man to live in alone.

However, now I shall come home to you there – at least, I expect so." And he smiled.

"Of course you will." She spoke quickly. "I'll keep everything as you like it, Nigel. I think I know the way you like to have things."

"I think you do," he agreed gravely.

There was another silence, and then he said:

"Val, I'm going to ask you to do something for me."

"Why, of course. Anything you like." She was glad to think there was anything she could do for him in return for all he had done for her.

"I want you to promise not to see Larry Bowdon any more."

Whatever she had expected, it was not that. She gave a slight gasp of astonishment, and then said almost coldly:

"That would be rather difficult, you know, in a place the size of Arden. I can hardly cut him dead – there's no real reason why I should – and I'm sure to meet him from time to time."

"I didn't mean that. You'll have to meet him casually, of course, and I agree there's no reason why you should ignore him conspicuously. But I meant – don't have anything much to do with him except as a matter of everyday courtesy."

"I don't know why you think it necessary to say that to me." Valerie was angry, and the slight tremor in her voice showed as much. "There may have been – unusual features about our marriage, but at least I shouldn't act unfairly when your back was turned. I think it's not very kind of you to suggest that I should."

"I wasn't suggesting it, Val." He took her anger quite

82

calmly. "But, though I may not know much about women, I know a good deal about men, and I don't like your Larry Bowdon at all."

"It isn't – necessary for you to like him. I suppose you hardly could in the circumstances. But I think you might do me the justice of believing that I should remember I was your wife – even when I am talking to Larry."

"I know. I'm sorry, I've put it rather badly. Perhaps what I ought to have said was that there is such a thing as playing with fire, and that the surest way to avoid getting burnt is to keep away from the fire. Don't think I distrust you, or anything like that, Val. I don't want you hurt any more, that's all."

Against her will she was softened.

"It's all right," she assured him quickly. "I expect I took it the wrong way. But don't worry, Nigel. Everything between me and Larry was finished before – before you came. He's nothing but an acquaintance now, and I should never treat him as anything else."

"Then there's nothing else to say," he told her. And if he thought that the vehemence with which she spoke had anything to do with her anxiety to convince herself, nothing in his manner betrayed as much.

They had a singularly sweet and peaceful day after that. It didn't seem like a wedding-day, but she enjoyed it none the less for that. They lunched at a pleasant country inn, drove slowly through the sunny afternoon, and returned to Monks Alder in time for an early supper.

The time seemed to go terribly quickly after that, and it was a very short while before Mabel was looking in to say:

"You'd best be getting down to the station now, you know. It'll take you all of ten minutes to the Junction."

Valerie stood up and said rather nervously:

"I'll drive you down, Nigel."

"You don't have to. Station farewells are always the very deuce. I can get the village taxi down, I expect."

"No, I'd like to come."

He made no further objection. And presently they were in the car again, driving through the quiet, darkening lanes.

At the station he gave over his luggage to a porter. Then, taking Valerie's arm, he strolled with her up to the far end of the platform. The Junction was countrified enough, in spite of its name, and as they stood there, away from the main part of the station, they might have been alone in the fields.

"Thank you, Val dear. It's been a wonderful day," he said.

"I thought so too. I – I'll write to you and tell you how much I thank *you* for everything."

"There isn't any need. But write anyway."

"Yes, of course."

There was the sound of the train in the distance. Then his arm was round her, and he was holding her close to him – as Larry had so often. Only, somehow, it was different.

"Good-bye, Val."

"Good-bye, Nigel."

Funny that they found nothing else to say at all.

There were an unusual number of people going by the train that night, but Valerie noticed none of them. She only knew that she had said good-bye to Nigel, that he stood smiling at her in the doorway of his compartment, and then that the door was shut upon him. The train moved off into the night.

She turned away and went slowly out of the station. As she passed the light by the barrier, a voice exclaimed:

"Valerie! Is that you?"

And, looking into the shadows, she recognised the tall, elegant figure of Larry's mother.

"Good evening, Mrs. Bowdon." It was an awkward moment. For one thing, Valerie was very conscious of not having seen Mrs. Bowdon since the break with Larry, and for another, she had no idea how much Larry had seen fit to tell her of subsequent developments.

But Mrs. Bowdon, whose manner was very seldom cordial, seemed unusually anxious to be agreeable, and, since she had to go home the same way as Valerie, it was impossible to do anything but offer her a lift in the car.

"Thank you, my dear. I should be glad of it. The buses are so irregular, aren't they?"

Valerie murmured that they were, and somehow concealed her astonishment, because she could not recall that Mrs. Bowdon had ever called her "my dear" before in the whole of their acquaintance.

It was possible, of course, that she considered Valerie "safe" now that she was married, and therefore saw no real objection to being something like friendly to her.

But after a few moments, Valerie decided that this was not the explanation. On the contrary, there was obviously something really worrying her, and for some unknown reason she wanted to confide in Valerie, of all people.

"You know, Valerie," she began with rather less than her usual cool calm, "I have been a good deal *worried* lately by the situation between you and Larry. I don't want you to think I would interfere in any way" – Valerie could not help thinking that this consideration had never weighed greatly with Mrs. Bowdon before – "but, as you know, Larry is all I have, and his happiness is my first concern."

She paused, as though inviting some comment.

Valerie was silent, however, biting her lip slightly and staring rather hard down the road in front of her. Then, as she saw she really had to say something, she spoke nervously.

"I don't know quite how *I* can help you, Mrs. Bowdon. I think you must know that Larry and I – broke things off more than a week ago, and –"

"That's just the point!" Mrs. Bowdon interrupted her eagerly, and there was real distress in her voice. "I know there was what I might call – trouble between you, and indeed, Larry told me that you gave him back his ring. But –" she hesitated, and Valerie saw that her pride, as well as her maternal affection, was having a bad time of it. "Valerie, I'm going to be quite, quite frank with you. I haven't always thought that you were perhaps the right girl for Larry –"

"I was aware of that," Valerie said softly and just a little dryly.

Mrs. Bowdon glanced at her with a touch of most unusual nervousness, and Valerie felt sorry at once.

"– But I'm willing to admit now that it is, after all, for Larry himself to choose." Valerie felt that this admission must have cost a great deal, and she would willingly have stopped Mrs. Bowdon from going further, but, having once decided to unburden herself, it seemed Mrs. Bowdon intended to do even this thoroughly.

"He has been quite a different boy this week," she hurried on breathlessly, "ever since his engagement was broken. I haven't known what to do with him. And then today – this afternoon – there was a very painful scene. He said a great deal about his life having been ruined and that – he was quite beside himself, poor boy, of course! – that I was responsible. I don't know what he could have meant, Valerie, unless it was that he thought my – lack of enthusiasm had helped to put you off. When I saw you just now I thought I must speak to you about it. I want to say that if this trouble is owing to anything that I –"

"Mrs. Bowdon, *please* don't say any more." Valerie was extremely agitated in her turn for, however little she liked Mrs. Bowdon, she certainly had no wish for her to sacrifice her pride in this way. "I'm afraid there isn't a thing you can do about it. Nor I, either. Evidently Larry didn't tell you the really important thing. I was married today. That was my husband to whom I was saying good-bye at the station."

"Your – husband?" Mrs. Bowdon gave a slight gasp. "But I had no idea there was anyone else."

"No. It was all very sudden." Valerie spoke rather curtly, and thought she had never realised before what a long way it was from the station to the Bowdons' house.

"But who is he, Valerie? Someone in Arden?"

"No. Aunt Evelyn's son. He came over from Canada some – some time ago."

"From – Canada?" There was a short silence. Then

Mrs. Bowdon asked one dry question: "How long have you known him?"

"About a week," Valerie said grimly. She had not realised until now how difficult explanations were going to be.

"A week." Mrs. Bowdon laid no emphasis on that – simply repeated it – but the way she did so reduced Valerie's actions to something less than contemptible. "Well, Valerie, I must congratulate you. You seem to be a very lucky and businesslike young woman. Please forget anything I said to you a few minutes ago. I naturally feel now that any – coolness on my part has been amply vindicated. Perhaps you would put me down here at the end of the road. You must not bother to come any further out of your way."

In silence Valerie stopped the car and opened the door for Mrs. Bowdon to get out. They exchanged a very cool and formal "good night." Then Valerie closed the door again with perhaps a little more force than was strictly necessary, and drove away.

"And that, my dear girl," she told herself grimly, "is what it feels like to be classed as a gold-digger."

The next few days were quite astonishingly uneventful – so much like many other days which she had spent year after year at Monks Alder that it was very difficult to remember that she was Mrs. Hanson now, not Miss Eaton, and that she was the mistress of the place, not just holding it temporarily until Aunt Evelyn should come back from a strangely long absence, or Susan arrive to take fretful possession of it.

The first letter from Nigel arrived towards the end of the week. He sounded cheerful and very much absorbed in his work, but he had not forgotten her practical concerns. The letter contained a substantial cheque in her name, and the information that he would of course be sending her a regular monthly allowance.

"I'm afraid there wasn't much time to discuss the important question of money, Val," he wrote. "We shall have to talk everything over in detail when I get home – whenever that may be. There are sure to be a good many formalities in connection with the estate before we shall be able to touch any of that, I expect – getting a grant of Letters of Administration and all that sort of thing, especially as there was no will. But no doubt we can scrape along on what I have until then. I'm somewhere in that vague region between a pauper and a millionaire. Let me know if there's anything that you need, and you shall have it."

Valerie smiled a little as she folded up his letter again. There was something very pleasant in the contrast between this easy generosity and the anxiety with which Gerald had scrutinised every penny of expenditure during the unhappy weeks she had spent with him and Susan.

She wondered idly how they were faring, and then remembered guiltily that she certainly ought to write to Susan and admit that she had committed no less an enormity than marrying the interloper. But it was remarkably difficult to know just how one could explain that, and the cool contempt of Mrs. Bowdon had been a very clear indication of how the uncharitable would regard her actions.

"I'll write tomorrow," thought Valerie, a little ashamed of herself for putting off the unwelcome task. It was so pleasant to lie here in a long cane chair under the trees that it was difficult to bring oneself to consider anything very earnestly.

Even when Mabel came out across the lawn, Valerie only greeted her with a sleepy smile and said lazily:

"Well, Mabel, what is it?"

"It's that young Larry Bowdon, Valerie. He seems determined to speak to you yourself – says he has a letter for you. Though why he couldn't give me the letter I *don't* know."

"Larry?" Mabel's first words had jerked her into almost painful attention.

"Yes. I told him to wait until I saw what you had to say about it, but" – Mabel gave an annoyed "tch" – "here he is coming from the house now."

"All right, Mabel." Valerie spoke with determined coolness. "I'll see him, of course."

Mabel turned away, grumbling a little under her breath, as Larry came up. He spoke without any preliminary greeting, hardly waiting even for Mabel to move out of earshot.

"I'm sorry, Val, to be so insistent, but I had to see you."

"That's all right, Larry." Valerie gave him her hand, though really it seemed silly and formal to be greeting him with anything but a kiss. "Mabel says it's something about a letter you have for me."

"Oh yes." He appeared to recall that with difficulty, dragging the letter from his pocket and handing it over as though it were not of much importance.

Valerie felt inclined to think that too when she saw the writing was Susan's. How exactly like her absurd cousin to address a letter to her at Larry's house! Even if she did feel sure that Valerie would have left Monks Alder by now, surely she could have made a more tactful arrangement than this? But of course, this probably was Susan's idea of tact – giving Valerie a chance to make some sort of connection with Larry again.

"Thank you, Larry." Valerie slid her thumb absently under the flap of the envelope. "It was good of you to bring over the letter personally, though I don't think it can be anything very important. It's only from Susan."

Larry made an impatient little gesture of almost literally brushing the letter aside.

"Oh, it wasn't about the letter that I wanted to speak to you."

"No?" Valerie looked up quickly, her attention arrested by the almost violent way he said that.

"Valerie" – he came and knelt on the grass beside her chair suddenly, taking her hand in a tight grip, whether she liked it or not – "it's about this horrible, iniquitous marriage of yours –"

"Larry, *please*!"

"How could you? You must have been crazy, darling! What does anyone know about this fellow except that he appeared from nowhere, and now seems to have cleared off just as mysteriously? What earthly proof have you that he's even the man he claims to be? Mother repeated to me what little you told her the other evening, and I haven't been able to think of anything else since. Why, Val, the man's a complete stranger! He may be a swindler or a bigamist or a murderer, for all you know. You *must* get out of this ghastly –"

"Just a moment!" Valerie interrupted so sharply that even Larry stopped speaking. "Please remember that whatever *you* choose to think about Nigel, *I* have married him. I don't think there's anything that we can discuss about that now."

"Married!" Larry made another of those impatient little movements. "You have a ceremony in the morning and he leaves you that evening. I don't call that marriage, and, thank God! nor would anyone else. That's your chance, Val. That's why I had to come and speak to you before it was too late. I don't know where he's gone, but—"

"He has gone on a business trip," Valerie retorted coldly, "and I happen to know exactly where he is all the time. I don't know quite what else you're insinuating."

"My dear —" Larry spoke more quietly now, and she noticed with reluctance how much more serious and earnest he looked than he ever had before. There was even something a little worn about him, as though anxiety had been teaching him a very sharp lesson. "I'm sorry if I'm putting things crudely and tactlessly. But I've been crazy with worry about you. I can't help knowing it's my fault more than anyone's —"

"Larry, *no*!"

"Yes, it is." He dropped a light, remorseful kiss on the hand he was holding, and Valerie felt her heart stop for a moment. "Do you think I don't know what a shallow, selfish sort of cad I was when you came to me the other evening? That instead of helping you and supporting you at a moment when you most needed me, I thought first of how difficult the position was going to be for me?"

"Oh, Larry, it doesn't matter now." But the little sigh

she gave was half happiness that she was hearing again the generous, frank and boyish Larry whom she loved so well. It was as though some sort of madness had passed, leaving him as she had always known him, and instinctively she put out her hand and ruffled his hair affectionately, as she had so often done in happier days.

"But it does matter, darling. What I did left you helpless and friendless – I can't ever forgive myself for not seeing things more clearly! – and that was why you took this mad and unnatural decision. I'm not proud of my part in this, Val, and I'm not going to make excuses about it. But will you try to understand that it wasn't easy for me, being almost entirely dependent on Mother – that it made me angry and nervous about the future, and that was why I failed you just at the moment when I ought to have had enough stiffening to take a firm stand?"

"It's all right, Larry." She spoke quickly, trying not to let him see how deeply his remorse moved her. "I do understand, and I don't really – blame you. Please don't blame yourself either. I don't want you to. Things just didn't work out the way we meant them to, and – well, that's all, Larry. There's nothing to be done about it."

"But there is! That's where you're wrong, Val dear. The situation has changed. This whole dreadful upset has changed it. I had a long talk with Mother. She sees now that I *must* have some sort of life of my own. Anyway, the upshot is that she has decided to make over a definite part of her fortune to me, rather than wait for me – well, to inherit it. I'm to be really independent, even without waiting until I get my degree. Don't you see what that means, darling?"

Valerie slowly drew her hand away, aware suddenly that it had become very cold in the garden – or else that she had grown cold.

"No, Larry, I can't say that I do – at least, not where you and I are concerned. I'm glad for your sake, of course." She wondered if he realised, as she did, how much of his mother's generosity was due to the fact that she considered him really "safe" now, and how much to her unkind desire to demonstrate to Valerie that she had thrown away what she really wanted, just a week too early.

But Larry was not thinking on those lines at all. He even laughed a little at her gravity.

"You dear little goose!" he said, and kissed her before she could stop him. "Don't you see that you and I can seal this horrible break there's been between us? I can do what I really want now – and surely, Val, it doesn't need me to tell you that what I really want is to marry you?"

"Are you forgetting that I'm already married?"

"But that isn't a marriage, I tell you."

"To me it is."

"All right, have it that way if you must. But it's the kind of marriage that can easily be dissolved. You don't *need* it any more, Val. You can't have entered on it for anything but practical necessity. Well, that necessity is over. Don't you see?"

"I couldn't, Larry. Nigel's been so good to me. It would be just about the meanest thing possible, to turn round now and say, 'Thanks, but I don't need you any more.'"

"But you don't owe him anything, dear."

"I do. I owe him a great deal of gratitude."

"Oh, Val! For something from which he expected to get his share of pleasure too?"

"That isn't the point."

"But, darling girl, what *is* the point? The man is practically a stranger to you, isn't he? He couldn't be anything else."

Valerie was silent, but as he pressed her for a reply, she finally said:

"Very well. I don't know him intimately, of course, but that doesn't really alter the case."

Larry got to his feet with an exasperated little laugh.

"If I didn't love you so much, I'd be angry with you," he exclaimed. "What *can* I say to make you see things as they are?"

Valerie didn't know. She watched him nervously as he walked a few paces away from her, his hands thrust into his pockets. In one way she wanted most terribly to agree with him, of course, but how could one behave shabbily to Nigel, when he himself had been so unbelievably generous?

She glanced down unhappily at Susan's letter, which she was still holding. In her agitation she had unfolded it, and now Susan's large, straggling writing stared up at her. There would not be anything of interest in the letter, of course.

Then one sentence, lavishly adorned with exclamation marks, caught her attention. A familiar name seemed to leap out at her, and she caught up the page eagerly.

"*Imagine!*" ran the sentence amid a forest of underlinings, "*that Nigel Hanson person has turned out to be a* complete impostor, *as we suspected. Geraldsays –*"

CHAPTER VI

LARRY was speaking again, eagerly and pleadingly, as though he thought he might convince her by sheer eloquence.

But she was not listening. She was not even making a pretence of listening. She was reading that one sentence of Susan's over and over again.

Only when Larry said, "Val, I don't believe you're paying the least attention to me," did she pull herself together. And then, curiously enough, her first overwhelming impulse was to conceal from him any hint of what she had just read.

Her composed smile was defensive, and it was deliberately evoked in defence of Nigel. He might be an impostor, as Susan so confidently asserted – it might be that she would find unanswerable proof of the fact in the other pages of the involved effusion now in her hand. But, guilty or innocent, sham or genuine, he should not be exposed at this moment to the triumphant scorn of Larry, if she could help it. He had stood by her when she had needed it. She owed him some sort of loyalty.

All these thoughts – in a somewhat confused form – took no more than a few seconds to pass through her mind.

The smile was accompanied by the faintest shrug, and she said:

"I'm sorry, Larry. Something in this letter caught my attention."

"Caught your attention!" Larry looked slightly bewildered. "Val, are you just trying to humiliate me by bothering about some casual letter from Susan when we were discussing our future together?"

"My dear, we have no future together," Valerie told him with great firmness. "I've tried to make you see that. If you simply won't listen to me, what else can I do?"

He looked at her for a moment in troubled silence, his hands thrust into his pockets, his eyes genuinely miserable.

"I don't blame you for wanting to put me through it," he began at last. "When I think how I –"

"Larry, this has nothing to do now with anything you did. I'm not being resentful or – or trying to take it out of you or anything petty like that. The plain fact is that I'm married, and my future is with Nigel."

"Val! – And he may be the most shameless impostor, for all you have evidence to the contrary."

She had an unpleasant little feeling when Larry said that word, and for a moment her hand closed tightly on the letter she was holding. But she answered quite steadily:

"I'm not going over that again. I think you must have said all that you want to say now, Larry. And I've certainly heard all that I want to hear. You don't mind if I go into the house, do you? I have several things I want to do."

"You mean" – he barred her path for a moment in a final appeal – "you mean that you're absolutely finished with me? That you don't ever want to see me again?"

"Larry, must you put it quite like that?" She was greatly distressed and unable to hide the fact. "Of course

I don't mean that I never want to see you again, only –"

"Then I *can* come here sometimes to see you? Oh, Val, you don't know what that means to me. It's all so – empty and cold and hopeless at home. I think of you all the time, wonder what you are doing and what I can do to show you how sorry I am. I keep on telling myself that anyone as dear as you *must* forgive me when I'm so sorry and ashamed, and then I remember –"

"There isn't anything to forgive, Larry. Don't blame yourself any more – please, please. It's only that – that – you mustn't talk as though there is anything between us any longer. There isn't, and – oh, let me go now!"

She turned away and walked rapidly towards the house, aware that Larry stood there staring after her, but making no attempt to follow her.

Only when she was in her room, and was nervously smoothing out the crumpled sheets of Susan's letter, did she realise that she had not been firm enough about telling him not to come to the house again. It had been difficult to know what to say in the agitation of the moment – but she ought to have made it clear that, while she had no bitter feelings against him any more, it simply was not *right* for him to come calling in at Monks Alder whenever he pleased.

Desperately fighting down the sensation of sick regret she turned back to the beginning of Susan's letter.

"*Gerald says that I'm not to say anything to you until we have* every *kind of proof,*" was how the letter actually began. "(*At least, I mean he said I was not to tell* anyone.) *But I feel you aren't exactly* anyone. *And you ought to know, Val. You're almost a relation, after all, and he might try to deceive you in some way and make more mischief."* Valerie decided that the "he" in this case was Nigel and not Gerald. The next paragraph confirmed this.

"It seems he's not Nigel Hanson at all. That is, his name is Nigel Hanson, but he isn't the person we think. We are not quite sure whether he meant to deceive us or Aunt Evelyn's husband meant to deceive her. These things never are so simple as they look written down," Susan added somewhat surprisingly.

"Gerald is determined to get to the bottom of the mystery, and then we'll show this person up. I know, Val, you will be just as glad as we shall," concluded Susan with touching, if misplaced, confidence.

"Ridiculous woman!" muttered Valerie. "Why should I be glad, I should like to know? The whole thing is some absurd mare's nest, I expect, built out of Gerald's spite and disappointment."

But she was shaken by Susan's certainty and jubilation.

"Do be careful of anything you say and do," ran a lengthy postscript. *"I don't know, of course, if you have already left the neighbourhood, but Gerald says he is quite likely to try to follow you up and make himself agreeable. He probably thinks it would be useful to get some connection with someone who was a sort of member of the family. Gerald says that kind of man doesn't stick at anything. That's why I thought you really ought to know now. You'd better destroy this letter, because if by any chance what I have told you were not true, I think it would be libel. But of course it is true."*

Valerie's immediate and very human reaction was to

decide that it was not true. Anything about which Gerald was so offensively positive simply ought not to be true. Besides, it would be so dreadfully unfair to have Gerald triumph over Nigel after he had come so generously to her rescue.

At this point Valerie pulled herself up, for she knew it was sentimental and morally unsound to argue like that. Either Nigel *was* an impostor (in which case, generosity did not enter into it), or else he was innocent, and Susan and Gerald were being stupid and spiteful.

That the possibility of their being right might mean happiness for her instead of tragedy was something she hardly dared to think about. Only, if Nigel *were* an impostor, and if there were an honest way out of this marriage which had gone no further than a ceremony, then she would be free to listen to the things which Larry had tried to say this afternoon – to think of the last fortnight as nothing more than a bad dream, from which there could be a blessed awakening.

But until Nigel's real position was established, loyalty certainly demanded that she should keep Larry at a distance. And one other thing was certain – Susan had better know at once how things stood. Nothing would be served by hiding the truth.

With feelings not untouched by grim amusement, Valerie sat down and wrote briefly:

"DEAR SUSAN, – *Thank you for your letter, which Larry brought over to me here at Monks Alder. I'm afraid you'll be surprised, and even shocked, to hear that Nigel and I were married last Monday. But you will understand that, in these circumstances, I hardly feel in-*

clined to pay much attention to your suspicions and insinuations. I'm sure you will realise" ("She won't, of course," reflected Valerie) "that you said absolutely nothing definite and offered no shred of proof to support your charges. That being so, I naturally feel more inclined to believe my husband's story than yours."

With a touch of mischief which she felt Nigel would have enjoyed, Valerie too added a postscript to her letter.

"I think," she wrote, "that perhaps you are right in fearing that your letter would be considered libellous if your statements are not correct."

Valerie walked down to the end of the lane to post the letter herself. But, once she had slipped it into the box, she turned back more slowly to the house, aware of a sense of misgiving which she had not allowed herself while she was writing.

What *did* she know about Nigel, when all was said and done? No one could pretend that his entry into the life of Monks Alder had been either conventional or calculated to inspire confidence. *Had* she really been little other than a gullible fool, ready to be exploited by someone who tried to ingratiate himself with the adopted daughter in the mistaken belief that this would somehow strengthen his own position?

He had been singularly anxious to have everything settled quickly, and he had made that curious request that she would not see and talk with Larry any more. Was that an effort to cut her off from someone who was bound to penetrate his schemes?

In all justice, Valerie had to recollect, the next moment, that there was every reason for the hurried wedding. His time had been short and it was essential that they married quickly or not at all. And as for what he had said about Larry – that could be explained, as he himself had explained it, by his genuine concern for her happiness.

As Valerie put out her hand to lift the latch of the gate, she saw that Mr. Ward was coming along the lane, and instinctively she paused, waiting for him to come up with her. It was just possible that the lawyer might know something, or say something that would clarify the present confusion.

"Good afternoon, Mr. Ward." Valerie stood there with her hand still on the gate, trying to think of something to say which would detain the lawyer – who seemed inclined to pass on. "I – I've been wondering if you have heard anything from my cousins. Mr. and Mrs. Manders, you know."

Mr. Ward paused, dug the end of his umbrella into the ground with a great air of concentration and said carefully:

"No, they have not communicated with me. There has been no *direct* communication, that is to say."

"What do you mean quite by that?"

Mr. Ward cleared his throat, as though wishing to give himself notice of that question before replying.

"I received by this morning's post a letter from Mr. Manders' solicitors," he admitted cautiously. "From Messrs. Foster & Foster. An excellent and old-established firm."

Valerie nodded hastily to indicate that she was glad they were an excellent and old-established firm and therefore worthy to do business with Mr. Ward.

"Was it about – Well, I suppose it was about the inheritance of Monks Alder?"

Mr. Ward showed signs of becoming even less communicative.

"I am not sure that I feel prepared –" he was beginning.

"But, Mr. Ward, this concerns my husband's affairs – my own affairs, come to that!" Valerie interrupted sharply in her anxiety. "Surely there can't be any breach of confidence in telling me."

"Well –" Mr. Ward, though slightly impressed by the argument, still seemed to find difficulty in realising that Valerie had any legitimate connection with Nigel Hanson's affairs. "Well, of course, that *is* a point. The letter was not a long one." Apparently he decided that, in consequence, its contents might be disclosed without danger, because, he went on, "It merely stated that Messrs. Foster & Foster wished to know if I were acting for your – ah – husband, Mrs. Hanson, as their clients, Mr. and Mrs. Manders, proposed to dispute his claim to the estate of the late Mrs. Hanson."

"And that was all?"

"That was all."

"They didn't say anything about the – the reason why my cousins were disputing the claim?"

"Naturally not, until they had ascertained whether I were indeed acting for Mr. Hanson." Mr. Ward was shocked. "It would have been a grave breach of professional etiquette."

"I see." Valerie sighed. She wished professional etiquette had not been quite so strictly observed in this particular case. "Then you have no idea what is behind this move?"

"I'm afraid not. I *assume* there is some question of doubting your husband's identity, but of course it is impossible to do anything but theorise at this point."

"Of course," Valerie agreed, and refrained from adding that she herself had been busy theorising for most of the afternoon.

"Perhaps, Mrs. Hanson, you would give me your husband's present address?" Mr. Ward went on. "I shall have to write to him asking whether he does in fact wish me to act for him in this matter."

"Yes, of course. Won't you come in? In any case, I'm sure he would wish you to act for him."

Mr. Ward's sense of professional etiquette received another slight shock at that, however.

"I should have to have instructions – *written* instructions – from Mr. Hanson personally," he said reproachfully as he followed Valerie into the house.

"Oh yes, I suppose so." Valerie wrote down the address for him. "This is where he is at the moment. It is the oil company's address, so his firm will see to it that all mail reaches him immediately."

"I see." Mr. Ward studied the address, then folded the slip of paper and placed it with great care in his pocket-book.

While he was doing so, Valerie watched him, trying to make up her mind whether or not she would take Mr. Ward further into her confidence. Then, as they picked up his hat from the table, she suddenly made up her mind.

"Mr. Ward, I received a letter from my cousin today –

from Susan. She seems to think they have evidence that my – my husband is not Nigel Hanson at all. I – should like to show you the letter." Rather hastily she pulled it from the pocket of her suit and handed it to him. "I'd like to know what you think of it."

Mr. Ward gave her a shrewd glance as he took the letter, which he proceeded to read with great attention. While he was reading it, Valerie watched him nervously, but she could not gather anything of his thoughts from his expression.

When he had finished it he folded it up slowly.

"I think," he said, "that Mrs. Manders is incorrect."

"In her suspicions, you mean?" Valerie was surprised that her own voice sounded so eager.

"Oh no, no." Mr. Ward shook his head. "There is no evidence one way or the other on that point. No – incorrect in supposing that her letter would constitute a libel."

"Oh –" Valerie laughed vexedly. "That doesn't really matter, does it?"

"Libel can matter a great deal – especially to the person who utters it," Mr. Ward assured her extremely dryly.

"Yes, yes, I know. But the real point is –"

"The real point, Mrs. Hanson, is that neither you nor I know anything like enough of your husband to hazard an opinion," interrupted Mr. Ward with unusual outspokenness. "You want to believe that there is no truth in this – this somewhat unbalanced communication from your cousin. Frankly, so do I. I liked what I saw of your husband. I had a good impression of him. And I am not a bad judge of character. At the same time, it would be idle not to admit that we are both being swayed to a considerable degree by emotion rather than reason in this feeling."

Valerie found it difficult to visualise Mr. Ward being swayed by emotion in any degree whatever, but, for the first time since she had known him, she felt her heart warm to the unexpected streak of humanity in him. It was good to have him say he liked Nigel. Somehow, it was extraordinarily good to have him imply that he hoped to find him innocent.

"Thank you," Valerie said, and gave the rather surprised lawyer her hand. "I feel too that there – there must be an explanation somewhere, even if I have nothing logical to back up the impression. I don't think I would even have admitted doubts to anyone else, but of course – of course –"

"Of course your marriage was arranged with somewhat disquieting speed," suggested Mr. Ward with a hint of severity. "And that naturally creates a feeling of – ah – uncertainty."

"Very well. That *is* how I feel about it. Though I know it's horribly disloyal of me even to speak about it."

"Thoughts are none the worse for being clothed in words," Mr. Ward said sententiously.

And as Valerie could find nothing to say in answer to this somewhat profound-sounding sentiment, there was a short silence, and Mr. Ward took himself off.

A few minutes after she had seen him out the phone rang. Valerie answered, and to her astonished delight it was Nigel.

"Nigel! The last person I expected. But where are you?"

"In London again. There's been a few difficulties and I'm back here again for more meetings. Look, my dear,

I shan't have time to come down to see you – I'm staying at the Excelsior – but I wanted to make sure all is well with you."

"Yes, everything is – fine." Valerie had no intention of bringing up a difficult subject over the phone, but already an idea was turning over in her mind. "How long will you be in England?"

"Perhaps two days. Now, my dear, I must go. Ring me if there's anything – and we'll discuss everything once this tour is over." And he rang off.

Before she had put the receiver down Valerie had made up her mind. She was going to make the most of this unexpected chance.

Within an hour she was in the train on her way to London.

By six o'clock she had reached the Excelsior, a small but very comfortable hotel off Piccadilly – very near the London offices of Nigel's company, she realised. Enquiry at the desk told her that her husband had not yet returned for the evening, but she managed to get a room for at least one night. Asking the clerk to let Nigel know of her arrival as soon as he appeared, Valerie went to her room to wash and change before going downstairs again to wait for her husband in the small lounge off the entrance hall. And then she began to have doubts about what she was doing.

Why had she come? Valerie wondered, in something like panic. If Nigel were indeed an impostor, then she was in for a most uncomfortable and humiliating scene. If he were not, then she was going to look a good deal of a fool – and face the crushing disappointment of knowing that the barrier between herself and Larry was as formidable as ever.

"Not that I *want* him to turn out an impostor," reflected Valerie unhappily, because suddenly the very thought of Gerald triumphing over a wordless and humiliated Nigel seemed the worst thing of all. But if not –

Then the door opened and he came into the room.

Evidently he had not received the message that she was there, because for a second he hardly glanced at her. Then:

"Valerie!" He crossed the room with a quick stride, and put his arms lightly round her. "Why, my dear? Whatever brought you here? Is something wrong?"

"No – no, nothing's wrong," she began quickly.

"Then do you simply mean that you came because you wanted to see me? But, Val dear, how enchanting of you! I had no idea you –"

"Oh, please!" She had to stop him before he got any further with that theory. "It wasn't quite the truth to say there was nothing wrong. I –"

"What then?" His voice was suddenly curt, and his whole air became purposeful.

"Nigel, I had a letter from Susan. They say they have proof that you're not Nigel Hanson at all. I had to come. I know it's ridiculous. I feel a fool even to be asking you, but" – she hesitated and somehow forced herself to look up at him – "you *are* really Nigel Hanson, aren't you?"

She saw his eyes narrow suddenly and the line of his jaw tighten. Rather slowly he released her, and thrust his hands into his pockets. He stood there looking down at her for a moment, then very deliberately he said:

"And suppose I tell you I'm not Nigel Hanson – what then?"

CHAPTER VII

VALERIE heard the sharp hiss of her own indrawn breath as she stood there staring back at Nigel.

"Then you *are* an impostor," she said slowly at last.

The slight touch of melodrama about that served to break his own grim tension, and suddenly he smiled and looked more himself.

"Not quite like that, Val."

"What do you mean? Either you're the man you pretend to be or else you've been deceiving us all. Why prevaricate like this? Surely it's simple enough to answer the one question? – Are you Nigel Hanson or not?"

He smiled down into her angry eyes and said quite deliberately:

"I don't know."

"You don't – *know*?"

He shook his head. Then, taking her by the arm, he said:

"Come and sit down. I see you and I shall have to talk this matter out."

Valerie sat down, never taking her eyes from his face. But they were no longer friendly, smiling eyes. They were grave and suspicious and angry. She felt as though she had woken fully now from some confused dream, to the realisation that she had been exploited by some plausible scamp, who still had the effrontery to try to deceive her afresh.

"I think I'd better warn you," she said dryly, "that I don't feel in a particularly credulous or indulgent mood. A little truth might save a lot of time."

"Oh, Val! That's a horrid speech. Worthy of Gerald himself."

But she refused to smile. At this moment even Gerald seemed commendably common sense in contrast to her gullible self.

"Suppose you just tell me the story."

"It involves a certain amount of family history."

"Very well."

"I don't know how much you know of your aunt's married life –?"

"Very little, except what Mr. Ward told me. That she and her husband separated after a few years and that he went to Canada, taking – taking their young son with him."

"Yes. That's right as far as it goes. On the plane going to Canada there was also a very great friend of my father's."

"A man?"

"No. A woman."

"I thought you said he fought shy of women."

"That was afterwards. Let me tell the story, Val."

She made a gesture for him to continue.

"They both had an unhappiness – a grievance – whatever you like to call it – in common. While he had a wife who was all too popular in the theatre world *she* had a husband on the stage and believed – rightly or wrongly – that he neglected her in consequence. I suppose it was the mutual feeling of being out in the cold that had first drawn them together. Anyway, the friendship seems to have been founded on real sympathy and to have gone very deep, at any rate with him."

"Were they – going away together to Canada?" Valerie was interested against her will.

"I don't know, Val. No one ever will know now. It is perfectly possible that she merely chose to build a new life for herself in Canada, particularly as she took her children with her."

"Oh – she had children?"

"Yes. A boy about my – well, the same age as Hanson's son and a baby girl some years younger."

"I see. And you think it was not unnatural for her to choose to go on the same plane as her very good friend?"

"Exactly." Nigel paused for a moment, and then went on with a little frown of concentration. "I don't know whether you know this bit, but the plane crashed. Hanson escaped and so did one of the boys. She was killed, but the baby girl survived. The girl was of course claimed by the woman's relations in Canada."

"And the boy?"

"The boy – myself, needless to say, either *was* or became Nigel Hanson. There was no one to dispute his identity, and no one to question Hanson's right to take him."

"But why on earth assume he was anyone but himself?" Valerie spoke eagerly, not quite able to explain, even to herself, the immense relief which came over her as she felt Nigel reinstating himself in her good opinion. "What should induce Mr. Hanson – apparently in his right mind – to insist that some strange child was his?"

"Not a strange child, Val. The child of the woman he loved – for certainly from letters found afterwards, he did love her – whether or not they were going away together. If he had lost both his own son and the woman who mattered most to him, it is conceivable that he took her child instead – all that was left to him of the disaster – particularly as the only alternative was that the boy should go to unknown relations."

Valerie bit her lip thoughtfully.

"Yes, all right, I do see the force of that. But why did it not rest there? I mean, why should the question ever have arisen?"

"In its present form?" Nigel smiled ruefully. "Because the sister – the baby rescued from the plane crash – has now grown up into a very inquiring young woman. I understand, from the little I have yet heard, that the story is that, on the death of her Canadian relation – or relations – she came across a box of her mother's papers and personal treasures. It had been rescued from the wreckage, examined no doubt at the time, and then set aside as being of nothing but sentimental value. The box contained not only letters but a diary – kept until the day of the crash. From various entries in this she seems to have gathered – I don't quite know how – that the boy who went with her mother's friend, Hanson, was probably her own brother."

"Nigel, what an extraordinary story!" She was no longer sceptical, only completely absorbed.

"Yes, it is. Quite exciting and pleasant if it didn't happen to be one's own story. The awkward part is yet to come. The sister – her name is Margaret – came to England much about the same time as I did, a few months ago. With a sisterly feeling, which I don't altogether appreciate at the moment, she set about tracing the English relations of her mother's friend. A pretty involved search brought her finally to your cousins' solicitors – at exactly the wrong moment."

"Oh, but how terribly unfortunate!"

"I think so."

"Have you seen her?"

"No. I received a letter from her. It was one of those sent on from Monks Alder. The only one."

"Why, of course! I remember now. I wondered who could already know that as your address."

"Well, dear Cousin Gerald supplied it, no doubt," Nigel remarked grimly.

Valerie looked straight at him.

"I'm – sorry, Nigel."

"What about, dear?"

She flushed.

"Oh – you know. Coming here full of suspicions – calling you an – an impostor and all that sort of thing."

"Well, so I might have been, for all you knew. I'm glad to see my wife displaying so much common sense."

"No – I'm serious. It seems so dreadfully mean now." Valerie looked really distressed. "To think of the names I called you! And all the time you were a perfectly innocent victim of an unfortunate misunderstanding."

"Now, Val dear, that's sweet of you to give me such a splendid reference. But – though I hate to be unworthy of it – the fact is that I can't claim complete innocence."

"Why – what do you mean?" She glanced at him quickly, thinking subconsciously that she had never seen anyone else whose eyes changed and lightened so when their owner was amused. "Have *you* had doubts on the question?"

He nodded.

"A few – and I must admit they seem disturbingly more than a few, now that I'm brought up against someone else's theories. I knew the story of the plane crash, of course. My father – I can't call him anything else – had often told me about it, and at some point or another I had gathered there was a very dear friend of his killed at the time, and that she too had had a boy my own age. I remember quite clearly that once or twice when I was a child my father called me by a wrong name – always the same name. 'Martin' instead of 'Nigel.'"

"But people often do that. I mean, think of two people who have often been together and use the wrong name."

"Yes, I know. And, taken alone, it wouldn't mean anything, of course. But not long before he died – he wasn't quite himself – he talked quite a lot about those days. I think he imagined he was talking to her, because he said more than once, 'Don't worry, Jean, I'll take the boy. I know it's what you would want.'"

"O – oh. That does sound rather more conclusive."

"Um-hm."

"So that when you came to Monks Alder that time, you already knew there were some doubts about your identity?"

"Yes."

There was a short pause.

"May I say something rather severe?"

"Of course."

"I think it was rather – cool of you in the circumstances, to come down there with the idea of demanding the place and saying nothing about any doubts on the subject."

He smiled at her.

"I didn't come down there with that idea. I came to see how things were and what my so-called relations were like."

"But you simply *rushed* in and claimed the place," Valerie protested. "Think how you hustled Susan and Gerald out!"

"And think what Susan and Gerald had been doing."

Valerie's eyes slowly opened to their fullest extent.

"Do you mean – You can't mean you did it because of *me*?"

He laughed a good deal at that, and leaning forward, took both her hands in his.

"Listen, Val. I found two perfectly poisonous people exploiting the misfortune of someone whom I liked –"

"You'd only just met me!"

"Don't interrupt. I liked you. I had it in my power to reverse the position entirely. The only argument against my doing so lay, at the time, in some vague doubts which might have absolutely no foundation. The really urgent thing was to get rid of Susan and Gerald and re-instate you in your rightful home. I didn't think it was the right moment to raise doubts on my own claim."

"Nigel, you're incorrigible!"

"But it's ethically sound."

"I'm sure it's not ethically sound to do people out of a rightful inheritance simply because you think – quite correctly– that they're awful people. It's a swindle."

"A very small swindle." He grinned reflectively. "And excusable in the circumstances. Besides" – he became more serious – "I had only the smallest doubts about my right to the place. Gerald was not the ideal person to whom to disclose them, and certainly that moment was not the ideal time to do it. Believe me, Val, I should have brought the question up later."

"After you'd enjoyed the inheritance for some while!"

"Well, I wasn't going to see very much of my ill-gotten gains."

"Oh no," she put out her hand remorsefully and touched his. "I know. *I* was the one to gain by it. I am grateful to you, Nigel, for doing this – this extravagant thing on my behalf. But really, my dear, you shouldn't have done it. Think of the risk, apart from anything else!"

"There didn't seem much risk at the time, Val," he confessed. "And I don't know that there's much risk exactly about it now. I can still appear as you so charmingly described it – a perfectly innocent victim of an unfortunate misunderstanding."

"Yes, but how – humiliating. In front of Gerald, I mean."

"Worth it, Val." He thrust his hands into his pockets and leant back, smiling at her.

"Really?"

"Of course. One doesn't get a chance of playing knight-errant every day."

Valerie laughed, a little put out. But she said lightly:

"So that's what you call it."

"Well, it sounds nice put that way, doesn't it? And now, I suggest we have some tea while we talk things over a bit more." He rang a bell, and within a very short while, a tray of delicious tea was brought in.

"By the way" – Nigel spoke absently, as he watched her pour out the tea – "the long-lost sister – Margaret, you know – proposes to look me up here. I am told to expect her tomorrow. I gather she is a young lady who invites herself and feels certain of a welcome beforehand."

"Well, after all, she is – or she may be – your sister," Valerie pointed out.

Nigel nodded without any signs of brotherly affection.

Valerie glanced at him doubtfully.

"That wasn't –" she hesitated – "that wasn't, by any chance, the reason for your not wanting me to come up, was it?"

He looked genuinely surprised.

"No. Of course not, Val. You're very welcome to meet her, if you think she will interest you."

"But you *didn't* want me to come, did you?"

He looked at her with a rather complicated expression and said:

"It might be rather awkward."

"But why, Nigel?"

"Well, for one thing, my dear, the place is absolutely full up. If you stay here at the Excelsior, Val, I'm afraid –" he balanced his spoon thoughtfully on the rim of his cup "– I'm afraid you will be expected to move into my room."

"Oh." There was an awkward silence.

"We could perhaps get you a room somewhere else," he suggested at last.

"It would look rather – queer, wouldn't it?"

"Would that worry you?"

"N – not exactly. It would be more awkward for you."

"I can put up with that," he told her dryly.

But something in that made Val think rather fast.

"I don't think there is any reason why you should," she said coolly.

"You mean?"

"That – that, if you have no objection to my being there, I haven't either."

It cost her something to say that, and she thought he must have guessed as much, because he glanced at her rather strangely as he said:

"Thank you, Val."

They had quite a gay tea together after that. He told her a good bit about his work. And she gave him a very lively account of her interview with Mr. Ward.

"He's not a bad old fellow in a rather withered way," Nigel said with a laugh.

"No. At least he's on our side."

"At least he's *what*, Val?" He smiled straight at her in that way she found disconcerting yet attractive.

"Well, I mean –"

"No, don't change it. You couldn't have put it more happily. So you're 'on my side,' are you?"

"Well" – she coloured a little – "you wouldn't expect to find me on Cousin Gerald's, would you?"

"No, of course not. Only these new developments have rather changed things."

"I don't see they should."

"Well, for one thing, I'm no longer undisputed owner of Monks Alder. In fact, there's going to be a hell of a lot of disputing about it, from what I can see."

"Oh – yes, I'd thought of that."

"Too bad, Val. Because now you have less chance of living there than you would if you hadn't married me."

"I don't see that," she said obstinately.

"Well, it would have been reasonable to leave you in residence there while the two regrettable parties wrangled it out together. Now you're too much an interested party yourself – married to the False Heir, in fact."

She laughed.

"Well, we – we can make some other arrangement, I daresay." She thought suddenly of Larry, and the smile left her face. If she were not living any longer at Monks Alder, where would she be living? Certainly nowhere near him.

That was just as well, of course, but the thought of having it ruthlessly decided for her like this cost her a terrible pang. Why, only a few hours ago she had been toying with the idea that circumstances might somehow restore her to him. Now she seemed bound, more irrevocably than ever, to the man who was smiling at her from the other side of the table.

"Has another, very serious, aspect of the case presented itself to you, Val?"

"No," she said rather hastily. "Why should it?"

"Only that you have become very grave, all of a sudden."

"Oh, it's nothing. I – I was wondering what I should do with Mabel," she fibbed a little desperately.

"Oh yes – Mabel, who would hardly mix well with Cousin Susan, and still less with Cousin Gerald."

"No. She detested them both," Valerie agreed absently.

"Well, Val, let's see first what we arrange for ourselves. Perhaps – if the idea of your going back to Monks Alder is impossible, and I think it will be – then perhaps you would like a small furnished flat here in town, and you would need Mabel with you then."

"Nigel, you have the nicest way of disposing of difficulties."

He got up with a laugh.

"And you have the nicest way of accepting the solutions. Would you like to come for a walk in the Park?" He glanced at her critically.

"Yes, I should like it. I've been sitting in the train most of the afternoon."

Before they went out Nigel had a word with the booking clerk and arranged for Valerie's things to be moved to his room.

"They *are* pretty full," he told her. "The clerk was most grateful to us for suggesting it."

As they walked leisurely through Green Park he explained the working conditions of his own life at the moment.

"I shall be spending most of the next few months commuting between here and the Gulf, you know. I'm afraid it will leave you a good deal by yourself, Val." She noticed that now he spoke as though she were going to stay indefinitely, and resolutely she took her cue from that.

"I don't mind. And then, if we take a small flat, I shall have Mabel with me, as you suggested."

"Oh yes, there's Mabel, of course. She'll look after you."

"Are you so sure that I need looking after?" Valerie laughed.

But he gave her a serious, reflective look which had something very kindly about it.

"You're not quite well yet, are you?"

"Oh – very nearly."

"All the same, I think you need some looking after – and you might not want to have it exclusively from me."

He said that without rancour – as though it were simply an understandable fact which must be reckoned with.

"Oh, Nigel –" She laughed a little, but as though she were rather moved.

"What?"

"You're so – I don't know how to express it – well, you can be singularly tactful, for a man who goes about knocking down the people he doesn't like."

He laughed a good deal at that. But, although he made no further reference to his part in looking after her, she noticed that he took care not to let her go far enough to tire herself before he insisted on their turning back.

By the time they got back to the hotel it was dinner-time. After a hasty wash and change, Valerie went down to the dining-room to meet Nigel. He was already there, and hurried to escort her to their table.

Her gaze travelled the length of the room. Then suddenly her smile faded, and she gave a slight gasp.

At a table near the end of the room, studying the menu with rather gloomy attention, sat Larry.

CHAPTER VIII

FOR a moment Valerie thought she must be dreaming. Then the sudden silence of the man beside her told her that he too had seen Larry.

In a sort of nervous dismay she glanced up at Nigel.

"I – I had no idea he was coming here," she said quickly, defensively – for she saw for the first time that those light eyes of his could look very hard and angry.

"Hadn't you?"

That was all he said, and the tone was curt enough.

She felt irresistibly impelled to defend herself, and she would have broken into eager protestations, but at that moment Larry looked up and saw her. Putting aside the astonished waiter to whom he had been about to give his order, he came quickly down the room towards her.

He appeared scarcely to notice Nigel until he had come right up with them, and even then he accorded him no more than a glance of unfriendly recognition.

"Val! Thank heaven I've found you! I had to come."

"There was not the least reason for you to." Valerie's voice sounded small, even to her own ears, but the tone was firm. "You had no need and no right to follow me."

"I had to speak to you before you – I *must* speak to you now – right away."

She was acutely aware of Nigel – silent – beside her.

"You had better say what you have to say quickly then, Larry."

"Here? But, Val, we can't talk properly here. Where can we go in this confounded place and be private? I must speak to you alone." He didn't look at Nigel as he said that, but his meaning was insolently clear.

"No. You can say what you want to say to us both." Valerie spoke coldly, but the quiver in her voice showed how agitated she was.

"It's impossible!"

Then for the first time Nigel spoke.

"I think," he said quietly, "that my wife has made herself quite plain. She does not wish to see you alone."

"Your wife!" The bitter scorn of that was obvious in spite of the fact that Larry spoke almost in a whisper.

"Exactly. My wife," Nigel agreed pleasantly. And Valerie – remembering his handling of Gerald – recognised the danger behind the pleasant manner. "Suppose we try the lounge. It will probably be empty at this time in the evening, and we can finish this interesting discussion there."

With his hand lightly round Valerie's arm, he led the way, and, sure enough, the lounge proved to be empty.

"Sit down, Val." Nigel drew forward a chair for her, but he himself remained standing.

Larry, too, preferred not to sit down, and, turning from Valerie for the moment, he addressed himself direct to Nigel.

"Is Valerie not to have any private affairs simply because she has gone through a form of marriage with *you*?"

"Val is welcome to any private affairs she likes," Nigel replied almost carelessly. "But that has nothing to do with my seeing that she is not pestered. I understood her to say she had no wish to see you alone. In that case, she will not see you alone."

Valerie, knowing that queer, white look round Larry's nostrils meant furious anger, hastily interposed.

"Nigel – perhaps for a few minutes."

"Not," he said quietly, "unless you really want it. There is no need for you to be either bullied or coaxed into a discussion *à deux*."

"Very well!" Larry interrupted suddenly in a tone which showed that his anger really had got the better of him. "If you *want* to hear yourself described as you deserve, I've no real objection. But Valerie is going to hear the truth now, if I have to shout it in front of everyone."

"I see no necessity for that," Nigel assured him. But Larry had already turned to Valerie again.

"This man is nothing less than an impostor, Val – a common swindler. He's tried to do your cousins out of their inheritance, and he's shamelessly used you in the process."

"And since when," asked Valerie with spirit, "have you felt impelled to fight my cousins' battles for them? I never knew you so concerned for their rights before."

"Your cousins! I don't care a damn about them or their rights," Larry said with candour. "It's the way *you* have been exploited which makes me see red. Susan and her precious Gerald can look after themselves, but –"

"You, I take it, are going to look after Valerie?" Nigel's cool, amused interruption might well have served to fan the flame of Larry's wrath, but, instead, he suddenly got a grip on himself and spoke more quietly.

"Valerie was my fiancée until very recently. And, however much that position may have changed, I still feel I have a right and privilege to look after her if she seems to me to be in danger."

"Larry dear" – Valerie was touched, and the endearment slipped out quite naturally – "I know you mean nothing but my good. Only can't you see that my being married –"

"It isn't a real marriage, Val, and I want to rescue you from it before it's too late. This man is just –"

"Yes, I know. You've told me that already. But what makes you accuse Nigel of being an impostor?"

"Why, you see" – Larry spoke eagerly, as though in sheer relief that he had obtained a hearing at last – "half an hour after you had gone this morning Susan and Gerald turned up. They were in a fearful stew. Someone in Arden had written and told them about this – this marriage of yours, and they'd come down to see what could be done."

("And to establish themselves at Monks Alder once more," thought Valerie.)

"They don't seem to have got much out of Mabel except cheek, so they came over to see me."

"And you were able to supply them with all information," Nigel put in dryly.

"As a matter of fact," retorted Larry with icy crispness, "they were able to tell me a great deal more than I could tell them. You may like to know that your sister Margaret has turned up and so your little scheme for impersonating Nigel Hanson has fallen flat."

"Just a moment!" It was Valerie who interrupted that time. "I know all this, Larry, and –"

"You know?" Larry was thunderstruck, and he passed his hand over his forehead as though the situation had become too much for him. "You know – and yet you're here? Val, has this man bewitched you?"

"No." Valerie made that very curt. "But the facts are not quite as you think. Susan and Gerald aren't exactly disinterested parties, remember, and –"

"Nor are any of us," Larry interrupted a trifle bitterly. "Look here, Val – heaven knows I'm no friend of Susan and Gerald, but at least we do *know* them. We know they are your relations – even if pretty poisonous ones. But this man is an absolute stranger. He arrives with a cock-and-bull story which shows signs of breaking down the moment it's called in question. He persuades you to go through a form of marriage, with what even you must see is suspicious speed. How do you expect me to do anything but accept your cousins' story rather than his?"

For a moment Valerie was at a loss. For one thing, put like that, Larry's case did carry a singular conviction. Of course Nigel *was* something of a mystery, and the marriage *had* been strangely rushed, and certainly the explanation he offered when his story was challenged was improbable and melodramatic to a disquieting degree.

Abruptly she got up and walked across the room. She knew both men looked after her inquiringly, but she could not help that. She stood looking down into the fire, trying to bring some order out of her confused thoughts.

Was she being weak and disloyal to be once more doubting Nigel – who, after all, was her husband? Or was she just an obstinate little fool not to pay more attention to Larry, who loved her and had been willing

126

to risk this very unpleasant scene in order to prevent her entanglement with Nigel going further?

For several minutes neither of the men said anything. As though by common consent, they left the next move to her. When she turned to them again, Larry made a half step towards her and then checked himself. But Nigel made no move. Only watched her, with his curiously anxious eyes slightly narrowed.

"Nigel" – she addressed herself to him, nervously but with a desperate firmness – "if you don't mind, I *do* want to speak to Larry alone."

She didn't feel very happy about the way he raised his eyebrows over that.

"For your own peace of mind? – or because –"

"For my own peace of mind," she said quickly, and he immediately made a slight gesture of assent, turned on his heel, and went out of the room.

"At last!" The exasperated relief in Larry's tone showed that he thought he was going to have things his own way. But Valerie left him in no doubt about that.

"Please don't think I'm taking your side in this discussion, Larry. I only asked Nigel to go out because – because – Well, obviously one simply can't discuss whether or not a man is a cheat when he himself is standing there all the time."

"He was thick-skinned enough about it," remarked Larry dryly.

"Well, that's beside the point." Valerie spoke sharply. "What I wanted to say is –"

"Valerie, just a moment. Before we go any further at all, *I* want to ask something. You don't happen to think you're in love with this fellow, do you?"

"Of – course – not.". Valerie sounded almost scared. "He's been wonderfully good to me, and I couldn't possibly let him down now and –"

"Exactly." Larry drew a sigh of relief. "I was afraid you were going to pretend it was love at first sight."

"You ought to know me better than to think I would pretend anything," Valerie said. "But he is my husband, Larry – and a good husband. There's not a thing he hasn't done for me."

But Larry was hardly listening.

"Look here, Val. You're not a child. You know quite well that, as things are, this entanglement doesn't amount to more than a ceremony and a sense of gratitude. All right. For God's sake don't let it go further. If you start staying here in the same hotel – letting yourself be known all round as his wife, don't you see it becomes something quite different? Of course I know you haven't any intention of living as his wife –"

Larry stopped suddenly, aghast, for a deep flush had run up Valerie's neck and cheeks.

There was a tense little silence for a second or two. Then Larry spoke almost in a whisper:

"Val! I thought you said you didn't love him. I thought you meant you still loved me."

She wanted to say, "I do! I do!" But instead she put up her hands to her hot cheeks and cried angrily:

"Larry, will you stop reading something into everything I do and say!"

"I'm not." He spoke harshly. "But either you mean to live with this man or not. You can hardly expect me to be indifferent about which it is."

"I – didn't say I was going to live with him."

"Then why were you colouring? You aren't a prude who'd start blushing because we were talking essentials."

"All right. No – of course it wasn't that. I don't know why I'm letting you talk to me like this – or question me. But – well, I *am* sharing a room with him. The place is full and –"

"How do you know the place is full?"

"Larry! Stop being like a public prosecutor! Because he told me so."

"Oh. He told you that, did he? Well, I got a room in this hotel without difficulty. Now what do you think of the ingenuous and knightly Nigel? Having hustled you into a rush marriage, he wants to cheat you into – well, God knows what."

"That – isn't – true, is it?" She was very white.

"Of course it's true. I could have told you he was that sort of fellow without –"

"No, I don't mean that. I mean about the – room. Is it true that you – that you got a room here without any difficulty?"

"Certainly." And then, as she said nothing, he added almost tolerantly, "It's an old trick, Val. I'm surprised you didn't see through it."

"Please don't." She didn't speak violently any longer. She felt too tired and dispirited and – disillusioned, she supposed. It seemed a small thing on which to hang her conviction that Nigel had been deceiving her – this question of whether or not a room was free. But it had meant a great deal to her when she had agreed to share a room with him. It had been her acceptance of him as the man to whom she would trust herself and her future – the sign that she had finally cut herself off from Larry and the old life.

She raised her eyes slowly, and found Larry still watching her, this time with anxiety and concern.

"What am I to do, Larry?"

She felt suddenly unable to cope with the small immediate details of the whole horrid situation. Larry must tell her what to do – Larry, who seemed so willing now to be like his old self – directing, suggesting, solving any problem which came her way. She ought to be very glad, of course, that the old Larry was back again. But somehow, gladness was not her uppermost feeling.

"You don't need to worry, darling." Larry took her gently by the arm, and although she felt vaguely that she ought to forbid both that and his calling her "darling," she had not the will to do so. "I'll settle it all. We can't clear out from here tonight, of course, but you can have the room I've taken. I'll go somewhere else. Even if there's no room here, I can find somewhere else. You leave it all to me."

"I must speak to Nigel myself." She was oddly firm about that.

"Oh, Val! Is it necessary?"

"Of course it is." She felt something like nervous irritation with Larry for not understanding. "He's got to know that I've decided – that I – Anyway, I want to see him."

"If I send him in here to speak to you while I go and arrange for the change in rooms, will you promise not to let him talk you over again into some quixotic arrangement?"

"Yes, of course. And – Larry?"

"Yes?"

"Be as – tactful as possible about changing the rooms. I don't want –"

"Unnecessary embarrassment? Of course not, Val dear. You don't suppose I'd do anything to humiliate you in front of a hotel clerk, do you? As a matter of fact, when I inquired for you here, I said I was your cousin, and spoke of you with the air of being a close friend and relation. I thought I might need something of the sort later."

"Thank you, Larry. But I meant – I meant – don't do anything to humiliate *him* either." Larry's face hardened. "He's well known here," she explained rather pleadingly. "His friends and colleagues are always in and out. I don't want any talk or unpleasantness, even if he –" She stopped. Then she went on more firmly, "Perhaps it would be better for me to speak to him first – explain things – and then let him make the change."

But Larry was quite firm about that.

"No, Val, please leave this to me. I can manage it without any comment or unpleasantness, and I'll consider that skunk too, if that's what you really want. But I'm not having him concern himself with your affairs any longer. I'll find him now and send him in for a few minutes, but do make the interview as short as possible. You only make yourself miserable by trying to be what you call fair to a man who just doesn't know what fairness is."

When Larry had gone, she bent down to the fire to warm her hands, which she suddenly found were strangely cold. That wasn't true what Larry said, of course – about Nigel not knowing what fairness was.

Why, in some ways, he was the fairest man she had ever known. Unless, indeed, he had been deliberately playing a part all the time she had known him.

She sat down in a chair by the fire and shut her eyes. For the first time for some weeks she felt wretchedly ill again. She supposed it was all the excitement and the long day's travelling. At the moment she felt she would have liked nothing so much as to be able to go to bed in her room at Monks Alder and have Mabel fussing around her.

But she had forgotten, of course. Monks Alder was closed against her once more. Now she was just where she had been when all the trouble started – except for the added complication of this marriage which was no marriage.

At least – no, she reminded herself. Larry was different. Instead of being aloof and strange and unhelpful, he really loved her after all, and wanted most passionately to marry her, when she was free of Nigel. She ought to feel very happy and relieved about that, of course, but just for the moment it was difficult to sort things out and –

"You'd better drink this, Val," Nigel's voice said quietly, and, opening her eyes quickly, she found him standing beside her with a glass in his hand.

He made no attempt to touch her and, struggling into a sitting position, she said confusedly:

"I'm all right. I don't want anything."

"Yes, please drink this."

She took the glass obediently, and he bent down to put some more coal on the fire.

While she sipped the hot, peculiar but rather pleasant

drink which he had given her, she watched him surreptitiously, and even a little fearfully. In the firelight the strong lines of his face seemed more than usually marked, and she noticed that his eyes were quite unsmiling for once, and the line of his jaw slightly grim.

He straightened up again.

"Finished?"

"Yes, thank you."

She handed him the glass, and he went over and put it on a side table. As he came back, she noticed that all his movements were unhurried, but there was no lack of energy in them.

"Larry said you wanted to speak to me."

There was something almost casual about that, but it set her heart fluttering again.

"Yes. I –" She locked her hands together.

"There's no need to be frightened, Val," he said, and she found she very much wanted to cry.

"No – I know. I'm not frightened. Only it's difficult to explain."

"Then don't explain. Just tell me what you want to do."

There was something blessedly – crudely – easy about that.

"I want – to have my own room again. There is one. Larry is leaving his, and –"

"I know. I've arranged it. There isn't anything for you to worry about."

"*You* have arranged it?"

"Certainly." He smiled dryly. "You didn't imagine I should let someone else arrange about my wife's room, did you?"

She leant back and closed her eyes again, trying confusedly to imagine just how he had taken the matter out of Larry's hands. There were a hundred questions she wanted to ask, but only one struggled to the surface.

"Are you – angry with me?"

"No, Val, of course not. It would have been more – friendly of you, shall we say? – to have left that matter to me rather than to Larry. But this isn't quite the moment to take offence over the finer shades of meaning. You're tired, aren't you? – and not a bit well, and you wish you were in bed."

"Please – don't. You make me want to cry."

"But why, dear?" He still made no attempt to touch her although he called her "dear" and laughed in a way that somehow suggested she *was* dear.

"I don't know whether I'm being a worm – or just a guillible idiot."

"Oh, Val! What rotten alternatives. Just take it that you're neither."

"Nigel, why did you tell me the hotel was full – that I – I had no alternative but to share your room?"

"Because I thought it was the truth," he said quite simply. "It probably was at that moment. What is to prevent a room falling vacant just before Larry arrived? Does my whole character really hang on the letting of a hotel bedroom?" And he smiled at her with real amusement.

She looked away from him, wondering confusedly whether this were superb effrontery or absolute honesty.

"It was careless of me, I daresay, not to find out for certain," he added, "but then I didn't realize a husband had to make out such a strong case for having his wife with him."

She knew he was laughing at her now, and she didn't know if she were angry or strangely relieved because of it.

"I think," she said in rather a small voice, "that I'd like to go to my room now."

"You shall, Val, of course. Would you like a doctor, my dear?"

"Oh no, thank you. I shall be all right in the morning."

"I'll have supper sent up to you."

He made no mention about sharing it with her, and she wondered if he had simply accepted the fact that she didn't want to have much more to do with him, or whether he were being rather clever about it all and leaving her to herself purposely for the time.

Oh, it was impossible to tell! Especially when she didn't even know what she really thought herself. She only knew that she didn't want anyone else explaining anything to her, or telling her it was perfectly plain that she had been taken in, or that she only had to make a decision and everything would be all right.

She got up rather wearily.

"Good night, Nigel."

"Good night. Would you like me to take you upstairs?"

"C – carry me, do you mean?"

"Well, it wouldn't be the first time, would it?" His amused eyes reminded her almost embarrassingly of their first meeting, and she looked away quickly.

"No, thank you. I shall be quite all right."

When she got outside the room she felt it was mean of her not even to have touched his hand when she left him – not to have said one word of real explanation of her changed attitude. Yet he hardly seemed to expect it.

Oh well, that simplified things. The only point that mattered now was that she must reach her room without coming across Larry again. She felt that another discussion with anyone would finish her.

She gained the upstairs landing in safety, and found that a pretty, dark-eyed maid was collecting her things from Nigel's room.

"Oh – are you moving my things for me? Thank you."

"Yes, ma'am. The other room's at the end here. It's small but it's comfortable and I've lit you a fire." She talked all the way along the passage. "Mr. Hanson said you weren't well and you were to have everything just as you wanted. This is the room. Now isn't it nice? And you get straight to bed, and I'll bring you up some supper. There's nothing like something hot and good to eat when you aren't feeling yourself. What would you fancy now?"

Valerie said quite truthfully that she didn't know, which seemed to please her questioner better than any specific choice.

"No. I know. You just want tempting, that's what it is. You leave it to me. I'll bring you a nice little meal."

And she was as good as her word.

Afterwards, Valerie decided, there would be plenty of time to lie awake, thinking out what had happened. But almost as soon as the maid had gone out again with the supper tray, Valerie was asleep. And she slept quietly and dreamlessly until late into the morning.

As she came downstairs rather late next morning, she wondered for the first time where Larry was. She supposed he would be coming to see her soon – probably had already been at least once that morning.

The place was unusually quiet, but the big square entrance hall was full of afternoon sunshine, and the doors stood open to the sunny street beyond. Besides the clerk at his desk there was only one other person in the hall, and that was a girl who had just come in. A singularly brilliant and attractive girl too, Valerie thought idly, appraising the slim black trouser suit and the enormous red hat which topped it.

She turned at that moment, speaking over her shoulder to the booking clerk.

"In the lounge, you say? This door? No, don't bother to tell him. I'll do my own announcing."

As she crossed the hall, Valerie thought suddenly:

"The sister, of course! The long-lost Margaret."

With something between amusement and genuine curiosity, she followed the girl to the door of the parlour.

Looking in, she saw that Nigel was sitting sideways on the window-seat working with some purpose, as yet unaware of the girl's presence, and still more unaware that she herself was watching.

The next few seconds were oddly like a film – like something which didn't concern her at all, but which she had to watch.

Without a word, the girl came round within Nigel's range of vision, and stood there, laughing a little and obviously waiting to be recognised.

Nigel looked up, and Valerie saw surprise on his face,

followed rapidly by amused recognition and then real pleasure.

"Why – hello," he said, as he got slowly to his feet. "What on earth are *you* doing here?"

And then, as though she were too impatient to wait for any more words, the girl threw her arms round his neck and kissed him.

CHAPTER IX

VALERIE felt exactly as though someone had hit her between the eyes. Not only the astonishment of a blow, but the real pain of it too. Without a second's hesitation, she turned away and crossed the hall to the stairs again.

She hardly knew how she reached her room again, but, once there, she sat down on the side of her bed, trying to decide where this piece fitted into the sordid puzzle.

His sister indeed! Margaret! The sister he was supposed not to know – and there she was hanging round his neck like – well, like an old flame. And he had recognised her. Nigel, who had told her – among other lies – that he had no experience of women.

"What an utter fool I've been," muttered Valerie, and thought that hurt most of all.

But that was not what really hurt most. Only when she tried to comfort herself with the thought that now indeed she was free to go to Larry did she realise what the fierce angry aching of her heart meant.

She didn't want to go to Larry. She wanted to stay with Nigel. Not the unfamiliar, unreliable Nigel who was kissing that girl downstairs, but the Nigel who had carried her home through the woods, defended her from Gerald, saved her from disaster, and offered to be a faithful husband to her.

Why hadn't she realised it before? She had been incredibly stupid to play with her happiness like this. At least, no – that was wrong, of course, because she had been stupid to have been taken in by his pretence. All the dear and charming things he had done for her, and on which she looked back now so eagerly, were part of his scheming – moves in his worthless game.

Valerie gripped the side of the bed with her hands until the pain brought her slightly to her senses.

"Now what is the good of sitting here inventing explanations for yourself?" she demanded fiercely. "Why on earth should he be passing off someone he knows as an unknown sister? People don't do things like that. Elaborate frauds like that simply don't fit in with everyday life. Besides, he was surprised to see her. He was expecting Margaret – or whoever he intended to pass off as Margaret. Then why should he look surprised to see her?"

At this point Valerie tried to decide just how surprised he had looked. Was it real astonishment at the sight of someone he had not expected, or just surprise because she had arrived sooner than he had calculated? Oh, it was impossible to tell, of course, but one had to snatch at anything.

Then she might not be Margaret at all!

How ridiculous to have rushed away full of suspicion instead of doing the only sensible and dignified thing – joined them a few moments later and heard explanations all round.

Why, she might be anybody. A cousin – the daughter of an old friend. (Though she didn't look like anyone's cousin, of course. Still less like the daughter of anybody's old friend.)

"But what on earth has come over me, anyway?"

Valerie thought, half frightened. "How can it suddenly matter so much to me whether he kisses a girl or not?"

She knew the answer to that, however, even before there was a knock on the door and his voice said:

"Val, are you there?"

"Yes."

"May I come in a minute?"

"Yes, of course."

She moved over to the little dressing-table, and pretended to be busy with something there, so that he should not get a very good look at her face.

"Oh, you're up. That's good. Are you feeling better?" He stood just inside the door, smiling at her and not looking at all as though someone else had been kissing him.

"Yes, thank you. I'm quite all right again."

"Would you like to come downstairs and meet the long-lost sister? She's arrived."

For a moment Valerie could not reply at all. She leant forward to the mirror, pretending to arrange her hair, hoping he would not see that she had lost what little colour she had had.

At last she said:

"What is she like?" and she was surprised at the casual interest which she managed to simulate.

"Oh – rather charming really. Do come down."

Valerie drew a deep breath.

"All right, I'll come down. You go back to her. I'll be down in a minute."

Still she didn't turn round to look at him. But after a moment she heard the door close behind him.

With a little gasp she straightened up.

So she was rather charming, was she? The farce was actually to go on – was, in fact, being played out at this very moment. Susan – Gerald – Larry, they had all been right. Nigel and his smirking accomplice (Valerie found she was unable to think of her charitably) were a couple of common swindlers.

"I *won't* go down!" Valerie exclaimed aloud. But she knew, of course, that she would. She had to see those two together – decide for herself what there really was between them.

Valerie had never been a prey to jealousy before. She had too much common sense, for one thing and, for another, there had never been the slightest need for it where Larry was concerned. Now she knew exactly what was the matter with her. She was hotly, furiously jealous of that extremely attractive girl downstairs.

And why?

Because she appeared to be on more than excellent terms with the despised Nigel – the cheat in whom Valeri was supposed to take no more interest.

"What a silly, inconsistent little idiot I am," Valerie told herself angrily. "I *can't* want Nigel for myself. Why, it's only a few hours since I was planning how to explain to him that I loved Larry."

But she didn't love Larry any more. That fact was incredibly, breathtakingly clear.

Deliberately she tried to recall her feelings for him – tried to convince herself that, if she were to meet him now on her way downstairs, the scene between Nigel and that girl would cease to be important.

But it was useless. She wished him well. With a sort of devastating, impersonal goodwill she hoped he would not suffer much over losing her – but it all seemed rather unimportant really. Larry had become a background figure in her thoughts. Nigel had taken the centre of the stage.

Worthless, scheming, shameless he might be, but he held her now in a kind of fascination. Everything about him had a poignant significance for her. The way he smiled – the faintly arrogant way he dealt with opposition – his good-humoured contempt for Gerald and, yes, for Larry too – the firm, easy way he kissed her –

But there she had to stop and remind herself that she was not the only one to know about that. That latest kiss of his had not been for her.

When Valerie opened the lounge door once more they were both of them deep in conversation, and even as she came in they laughed about something. Not the polite, slightly self-conscious laughter of strangers, but the laughter of a joke shared between friends.

Nigel came forward to her at once, and the girl too got to her feet and stood there watching, with an air of cool criticism, as Nigel brought her up to be introduced.

With an effort Valerie steeled herself to hold out her hand and say with something like cordiality :

"How do you do? It's rather funny, isn't it, that we don't really know whether we're really greeting each other as sisters-in-law or not?"

The girl laughed lightly and agreeably, but she hardly more than touched Valerie's hand.

"Well, Nigel and I already feel like – relations," she asserted, with a touch of possessiveness which Valerie found singularly unwelcome. "Perhaps we shall soon feel the same."

143

Nothing in her manner, however, suggested that *she* was going to make any efforts towards that desirable end, and Valerie thought swiftly:

"She can't stand me. She's astonished and dismayed to find Nigel married. She didn't know about that."

The impression was as clear as if the girl had put it into words instead of just saying it with her fine, rather sulky eyes.

They were beautiful eyes, Valerie noticed with grim honesty. Dark and thickly lashed, with a peculiar lengthening at the corners which gave them an enigmatic expression. She was undeniably a striking girl. Perhaps not strictly beautiful, but with a charm and attraction which – Valerie saw – held Nigel's amused attention.

For his part, he seemed entirely unaware of the instinctive antagonism which had sprung into instant life between the two girls. He brought up a comfortable chair for Valerie, put her into it, and then sat down himself with every appearance of intending to enjoy the unknown "sister's" visit.

At first Valerie thought there could not surely be anything like normal conversation between them. Not while she knew they were deceiving her and they knew they had a part to play. But, as a matter of fact, she almost immediately found herself making conventional inquiries and comments, and if one or two were made with the deliberate intention of seeing their effect, neither Nigel nor Margaret seemed aware of the fact.

Inevitably, of course, they spoke of the curious circumstances which had brought them all together (or were supposed to have done so), and Valerie said:

"When did you first have the idea that my husband" – she had never called him that until this moment – "was perhaps your brother?"

"Um?" Margaret brought her glance away from Nigel and fixed her attention on Valerie with difficulty. "Oh – when I – when I found my mother's diary, you know."

"Where *is* this famous diary?" Nigel inquired at that moment, with a good deal more amusement than Valerie felt the occasion warranted.

"Well, I – haven't it with me, of course."

"Not? I should have thought you would certainly bring it for your long-lost brother's inspection."

"I – left it with the lawyers."

"With Gerald's wretched lawyers? Oh, Margaret, that was too bad! I bet they're chewing over every word with their objectionable client. Don't you think so, Val?"

"I suppose so." Her voice was toneless and she couldn't, for the life of her, make it anything else.

It was quite characteristic, of course, that he should play out any farce with gusto, but the idea that he should find amusement and pleasure in deceiving her brought a sudden lump into her throat.

He glanced at her, she knew, and there was momentary anxiety on his face. So even he *did* have a few misgivings!

Almost immediately afterwards he ordered coffee, and she hoped neither of them noticed that her hands were trembling as she poured out.

"What are your present plans, Margaret?" he inquired after a while, and Valerie had the impression that he really didn't know them in advance.

"We – ell, they're a bit vague at the moment. I haven't any relations in England, of course – except you." She smiled straight at Nigel, and evidently excluded relations by marriage from her calculations. "When I arrived here and saw what a charming place it was, I began to wonder if I'd stay here – at any rate for a short while."

It was all rather inconsistent and confusing, Valerie couldn't help thinking. On the face of it Nigel did seem quite unaware of her previous movements or her future plans, which certainly argued that he had had no idea it was she who would turn up.

But then that greeting –! That was no greeting between people meeting for the first time. Whatever else was in doubt, one thing was certain. He had known Margaret very well at one time.

"There isn't any real reason why he shouldn't," Valerie told herself mechanically, but it gave her little comfort.

It was almost a relief when one of the staff came in and told her in a low voice that there was a gentleman waiting in the hall to speak to her.

She had somehow forgotten all about Larry, and for a moment she looked completely puzzled. But Nigel must have heard the message, low-toned though it was, and he was in no doubt about the visitor's identity, and she saw the line of his jaw tighten.

Larry was walking up and down the hall, his hands thrust into his pockets, and his whole air suggested that though he was agitated, he was anxious not to show it.

He gave a relieved smile when he saw her, and caught her by the hand.

"Val dear! I'm so thankful to see you. I couldn't get

146

hold of you again last night."

"No, I know. I went straight to my room."

"And then when I phoned this morning they said you were not to be disturbed."

"No. I – got up late."

"I see. Let's go in here and talk."

He led the way into the dining-room. There were several groups of people dotted about the room, having coffee or talking, but Larry found them a corner seat that was more or less secluded.

"It's not too private, though," thought Valerie with relief. "At least he can't start kissing me."

And then she wondered if it were really she who was thinking of Larry in these terms.

He, however, evidently had no inkling of her thoughts, because he plunged immediately into his own plans and ideas.

"Val dear, I've done nothing but think out this problem since I left you last night, but I've got it all worked out now. Of course it's perfectly simple. I don't know why I didn't think of it before. You must come home with me to Mother."

Valerie thought there were few things she would find less welcome, and perhaps her dismay showed in her face, because he rushed on at once:

"I know there were one or two hard words between you a little while back, but that's all over now, Val. You don't need to remember those now. Mother's house is the *obvious* place for you to stay, until you can get rid of this fellow and marry me."

Valerie couldn't help remembering how desirable this very suggestion had once seemed to her. Now it seemed impossible, and she said rather hastily:

"Thank you, Larry, but – but I don't think I should want to do that."

"But why not? Where else would you go, Val? I'm afraid Susan and Gerald will be going straight back to Monks Alder."

"I'm sure they will," Valerie agreed dryly.

"Well then – there you are. You'll have to come home with me. Besides, think how I shall love having you there."

She glanced at him in worried appeal.

"Larry, I don't think your mother would like it."

But she knew that was not her real reason. And she knew *he* knew it too. She saw an expression of incredulous anger and dismay come over his face.

"Val, you haven't some idea of *staying on here*, have you?"

She thought of Margaret with her arms round a laughing Nigel, and hastily said:

"No!"

"Then what do you mean to do, my dear?"

"I don't know."

Valerie gripped her hands together and looked away out of the window. She didn't want to face Larry's anxious, suspicious eyes. And, above all, she didn't want to be pressed to make a decision at this moment.

"Has he been trying to persuade you to listen to him again?" Anger began to show in Larry's voice.

"No. He never makes any attempt to persuade me."

"Then I don't see what the trouble is."

Valerie was silent. It seemed to her that life nowadays consisted of facing unwanted alternatives, and finally be-

148

ing pushed into taking the less unpleasant. If she left Nigel now – and of course she couldn't stay with him after what she had seen and what she knew – then she was immediately up against the grim problem of how to live. Larry said there was only one place where she could go, and she was horribly afraid Larry was right. But if she went with him to his mother's house now, it was a tacit agreement that she would marry him later, as soon as she was free from this present marriage.

"Oh, Larry – I *can't* decide all in a moment. It's quite impossible."

"But, my dear, you've got to decide some time, and certainly you can't just wait about here, trying to make up your mind."

That was true, she knew, and the reasonableness of Larry's voice dismayed her. It seemed to bring her decision nearer, for how *could* one go on saying "no," when it was all so obvious and simple?

"Don't you see, Val, that every hour you stay here with him involves you further? I hoped you were going to come away with me this morning – and now it's too late to go today. You simply must make up your mind now, you know, and let us get away in the morning."

"I – have – until tomorrow," she said in a small voice, rather like a little girl who had been pushed into a corner. "I needn't really decide until then, need I?"

Larry made a little movement of impatience.

"I don't know why it's so difficult, Val. I suppose you still have some lingering feeling that you're not being fair to the fellow. I assure you, you are doing him a great deal more than justice. He doesn't deserve your consideration in the least. But, of course, if you don't want to come to a decision until tomorrow there's nothing I can do to force you."

"No. Nothing," Val agreed, in not quite such a subdued tone. "I'm sorry to be so – so spineless and undecided, Larry, but" – she bit her lip suddenly – "it is *my* life, you know."

"I know. I'm sorry, too, if I sound impatient. I'll come in the morning, Val, and you shall tell me then that you're ready to come with me." Evidently he couldn't seriously entertain the idea that she would come to any other decision.

She managed to persuade him to go soon after that, on the plea that she was tired and meant to go back to her room. But when she got back to her room, she felt very far from resting.

She ought to have gone to say good-bye to Margaret, of course, but she felt unable to face those indifferent eyes again. Nigel would have to make what excuses he could – say she was not well, or anything else he liked. She didn't really care – for Margaret cared less than nothing about *her* existence.

About an hour later there was a knock on her door, and even before she said "Come in" she knew it was Nigel.

He came into the room, closing the door behind him, and said at once, "Aren't you well again, Val?"

"I'm all right. I'm just – tired. I thought you wouldn't mind making my excuses to Margaret."

"No, of course not. Are you sure you're all right?"

"Quite sure, thank you. What did she decide to do in the end?"

"Do?" He looked vague.

"Yes. Margaret. Is she going to stay on here?"

"Oh –" He looked faintly put out – the only time she could ever remember his doing so. "Yes. She seems to think she'd like to stay in town for a day or two."

"Oh."

"Val – you don't – mind, do you?"

"Not in the least. Why should I?"

"Nothing. That's all right, then." But he looked disturbed. Then, glancing quickly at his watch, he said, "I must go, my dear. I'm due at the Airways terminal."

"Very well."

"Val" – he came a few steps nearer – "we've *got* to have some sort of talk together, haven't we?"

"Yes."

"As soon as I get back from this trip – probably in three days' time."

"Yes. That will be all right." For the life of her, she could not make her voice sound anything but flat and cold, and he made no attempt to come nearer to her. After a moment he said:

"Good-bye, Val."

"Good-bye."

For a moment he seemed as though he were going to say something else. Then, turning abruptly on his heel, he went out of the room.

Well, that finished it!

Margaret was going to stay, was she? Of course they had arranged it together after she had gone out of the room. She had been a fool to suppose they would do anything else. But anyway, it settled things at last.

It had been absurd ever to have had any doubts on the matter. She'd been tricked and deceived and fooled enough. Now she was going to cut all that out – go back to Larry – pick up the old life where she had dropped it – and thank Heaven that, unlike most people, she had been given a blessed second chance.

"I don't know what Nigel's game really is," she told herself angrily, "but I do know it's something discreditable. Does he really suppose he can have me hanging around here and some other girl parked in the middle distance too? No experience of women indeed! It looks more like the other extreme to me."

Her anger sustained her for most of the lonely evening, but when she was in bed her thoughts kept going round and round in miserable circles.

She found herself making excuses for Nigel one moment, and angrily demolishing them the next, and when she finally fell asleep it was to dream that Nigel and Margaret were secretly married and were really laughing at her. In the dream he kept on saying, "It isn't a *real* marriage, Val" – just as Larry had done so often.

Perhaps the dream helped her to make up her mind. At any rate, when she woke up, her first thought was:

"I'm going to end it all with Nigel. I've made up my mind at last."

It was a singularly bright and sunny morning when she came downstairs. A morning calculated to raise any spirits and to make even those facing difficult decisions feel that perhaps the difficulties were not so great after all.

She had breakfast alone, then sat musing over her coffee while she decided what to do with herself for the next day or two. About the coming talk with Nigel she did not allow herself to think. The situation *would* be over some time, and she would go away with Larry, and everything would one day be as it had been.

Or would it?

Valerie sighed, then looked up as a smartly dressed, middle-aged man walked down the dining-room and stopped at her table.

"Mrs. Hanson?"

She nodded, but suddenly her heart knocked unpleasantly against her ribs with some vague premonition of disaster.

"May I sit down?" Again Valerie nodded, and the man took the chair opposite her. "I'm Robert Edwardes, Mrs. Hanson, and I'm a director of your husband's company. I take it you haven't heard the news this morning?"

"No – o." She felt suddenly cold.

"I'm afraid I have bad news for you, Mrs. Hanson, but someone's got to tell you. The London office had official notification half an hour ago. I'm terribly sorry, but your husband's plane is missing in the Persian Gulf."

CHAPTER X

For perhaps five seconds Valerie stared at him in absolute silence. Then she said, almost in a whisper:

"It's not true. It *couldn't* be true that anyone so alive as Nigel could suddenly be –"

"Don't say the word," Robert Edwardes exclaimed quickly, "and please don't even think it so long as there is any alternative."

"Is there any alternative?" Valerie cleared her throat nervously, but it didn't seem to make her voice any less husky.

"Yes, of course." He was emphatic about that. "The plane is only missing – there's no report of a crash. It may only have had to make a forced landing somewhere –"

She didn't know that she was sitting there drumming her fingers on the table, and she had forgotten Robert's presence until he said:

"I'm horribly sorry, Mrs. Hanson. We think the world of Nigel too, you know. It's very brave of you to take it so quietly."

"It was brave of you," Valerie said, "to come and tell me. It couldn't have been easy." And she smiled gratefully at him.

He patted her hand a little awkwardly and looked sympathetic.

"Try not to worry too much, Mrs. Hanson. It's a rotten business for you, I know, but 'no news is good news,' you know, and any minute something definite may come in. I needn't tell you that we're constantly in touch with the airline people, and the moment we hear anything more we'll be in touch with you." He stood up. "Will you forgive me? – I must go now. But I'll see you again soon."

She lingered on alone at the table in the breakfast-room window, because her mind literally refused to prompt her to do anything else.

She had not been sitting there more than a few minutes, however, when the door opened again, and this time it was Larry who came into the room. He glanced round, seemed relieved to see her there alone, and came straight over to her.

"Morning, Val. Got rid of him at last?" he inquired with an air of satisfaction.

"Oh, whom?" Valerie said stupidly.

"Eh?" Larry looked slightly startled. "Of Nigel, of course."

"Nigel," Valerie said deliberately, "is missing." She could not – would not – bring herself to put into words the idea that he might be dead.

"Missing?" Larry looked astounded. "How can he be? How do you know?"

"I've just heard. His plane is missing, somewhere in the Persian Gulf."

"Oh, I'm – sorry." Larry spoke awkwardly.

"*Sorry!*" Valerie felt she had never heard a more ridiculous or inadequate comment. "Sorry? Oh, Larry, how very nice and generous of you."

He looked restive.

"Well, frankly Val, you can't expect me to go into

ecstasies of grief about it, can you? I *am* sorry – I don't wish the chap any ill, but it would be ridiculous to pretend I'm heartbroken or that this alters anything that we arranged last night."

"We arranged nothing last night," Valerie said in a cold little voice.

"Val! You're not going over all that again, surely, are you?"

"No. I agree we've gone over it often enough, and I see now that I've been stupid and weak and unable to make up my own mind. It's my fault, Larry, that things have dragged on in this way. I haven't been fair to you and I haven't been fair to Nigel. It's taken this – this disaster to show me what a weak little drifter I've been, and now –"

"Val! For heaven's sake! There isn't any need to blame yourself like that. I don't know that I'm specially proud of my part in the beginning, and as for this other chap –"

"All right, Larry. You've said yourself that we've gone over it all too often as it is. I agree. I'm just going to tell you the one thing now that matters. I would have been honest and told you before, only I didn't realise it myself until yesterday. It's Nigel I love."

"You must be crazy!"

"No. At least, I don't much care whether I am or not. Whatever his faults are – and, to be absolutely frank, I don't *know* what they are – I love him. If – if he – comes back I want to be with him. If he doesn't want me – that's a different matter. But I've done with pretending to myself, and trying to decide what is wise, and listening first to one person and then another. Everything else

156

is just a side-issue – the only reality to me is that I love him."

Larry made a movement to interrupt her, but she put her hand on his arm to stop him.

"No – just a moment, until I've finished. I'm sorry if you're hurt and disappointed, and I know you meant nothing but my good when you followed me down here. But there's only one thing you can do for me now – go home and get over me as soon as possible."

Larry got slowly to his feet, a little as though he were not quite aware of what he was doing.

"Then you mean there's absolutely nothing else to say?"

"Nothing, Larry."

"And it makes no difference that this man is almost certainly a swindler?"

"No difference at all. But anyway, I think you've got that wrong somewhere. It's something on which we shall have to agree to differ. Something which can't be decided until – until I know what's happened, one way or the other."

After a moment he said:

"Do you mind if I ask what you intend to do? I mean, what your immediate plans are."

"I don't mind your asking at all, but" – she shrugged slightly – "I can't make any real plans. I think I'll stay on here for a day or two."

"Yes, I see." Another slight pause. "You will let me know if there is anything at all that I can do for you, won't you?"

"Yes, Larry, I will let you know. But I don't expect there will be anything." She made that sound final because she knew that was the kindest thing, rather than let him keep a few lingering hopes.

"Well, then" – he spoke rather awkwardly – "I think – I'd better go."

She nodded. At that moment, anxious though she was to end things, she felt very forlorn. He had been a good deal to her once – just now he seemed her only friend – but the time was past when she could expect to lean on someone simply because they *had* been good friends once.

"Good-bye, Val."

"Good-bye."

By common consent they shook hands, making no attempt to kiss each other, but it was a very sincere handshake.

And then he was gone, without looking back, leaving her to make what she could of her life alone.

It was a strange day, after that. She went out for a walk because there seemed nothing else to do, and all the time she could not get rid of the feeling that she was waiting.

She went upstairs immediately after lunch – and then wondered why she had come up to her room. It was rather dreadful here by oneself, knowing that, whatever happened, Nigel could not come knocking on the door with his casual but kindly advice, his strangely sincere concern about her health, or even – yes, she could have welcomed that – his lies about Margaret.

"It's only at a time like this," thought Valerie, "that one really discovers what is important and what is not. I wouldn't care about his kissing Margaret, or about his not telling me the truth, or anything at all, if only he'd knock –"

And at that moment there was a knock on the door.

With a sort of superstitious certainty that it *must* be news of Nigel, Valerie swung round from the window.

"Come in!" She could hardly get the words out.

But when the door opened it was only one of the maids who came in, and the sick wave of disappointment which came over her told Valerie more surely than anything else could have done how much Nigel meant to her now.

"There's a lady to see you downstairs, madam."

"A lady?" Valerie was puzzled.

"Yes, madam. A young lady – very smart and nice-looking, but she's ever so upset at the moment."

"Oh!" – Valerie realised suddenly that of course it must be Margaret – "I think you'd better show her up here, since you say she's – she's so much upset."

"Yes, madam."

The maid went out again, and Valerie was left to wonder how Margaret had discovered the news and – still more – just how much it meant to her.

She was not left long in doubt. It was an agitated and very different Margaret who was shown into the room from the smiling, self-assured girl of yesterday.

"Oh, do tell me" – she didn't even wait to take Valerie's hand – "is this dreadful, dreadful news really true?"

"I'm afraid so," Valerie said slowly, wanting, in that moment, to be kind even to Margaret, but faintly embarrassed that she seemed to take it upon herself to be even more agitated than Nigel's wife.

"You mean he's *dead*?"

"No!" Valerie's tone was suddenly fierce and cold.

"Don't speak of him like that. The plane has almost certainly made a forced landing somewhere."

"Do you *know* that?"

"No, of course not. One never does know these things for certain," Valerie said rather wearily.

"Then how can you be so calm?" Margaret threw threw herself down into the armchair by the window and began pulling nervously at the corner of the expensive-looking handkerchief she was holding.

"One just has to – try to be calm, I suppose. I think I'd only feel worse if I let myself go."

"Oh, that's because you're such a cold person. It's different with me. I – I don't know what I shall do about it."

Valerie was silent, very seriously tempted to point out that it was not necessary for her to do anything about it – that in fact she was behaving in a very tasteless and extraordinary manner. After a moment she said, with an effort:

"I know it's terrible, but try – do try to be hopeful. It – it isn't easy, I know, but –"

"Oh, it's all right for you," Margaret broke in impatiently and rather astonishingly. "You're only the girl he married in a hurry – I know all about that – but I – I love him." She looked defiantly at Valerie as she said that.

"I'm sorry." Valerie's voice was very soft and very cool. "I don't think I want to – wrangle about Nigel with anyone. But perhaps if you will try to remember that I am his wife, you'll find it easier to control yourself."

"I don't *want* to control myself." Margaret put her face in her hands suddenly in utter dejection. "I could just cry and cry if I really let myself go." Valerie hoped grimly that she would not really let herself go. "It seems so *hard* when I've only just found him again."

"You do know, don't you," Valerie said dryly, "that for a long-lost sister, you are rather overdoing things?"

"Sister?" Margaret raised her head and looked surprised.

"Well, you're not his sister, of course, are you?"

"No." Margaret shook her head impatiently, almost as though it were ridiculous even to waste time talking about it.

"Then do you mind telling me who you are?"

"I have told you. I'm the girl he loves."

"No, you didn't say that. You said you loved him," Valerie corrected her ruthlessly.

"It's all the same thing."

Valerie thought it was very different but felt unequal to arguing the theoretical point at that moment. She looked at the dejected figure of Margaret, and somehow found it in her heart to be sorry for the girl. After all, she too was genuinely grieving for Nigel, and Valerie knew only too well how wretched that state was.

"I wish," she said quite gently, "that you would tell me how you and Nigel *really* met."

"All right, I don't mind." Margaret was pulling at the corner of her handkerchief again. "It was in Montreal."

"Before he came over here?"

"Yes, over a year ago." Margaret sighed, as though recalling something very pleasant but very far in the past. It made Valerie bite her lip with vexation and real pain.

"And you – fell in love then?"

Margaret nodded.

Valerie immediately wished she had had the courage to put the question – "You *both* fell in love?" But she had not been able to summon the resolution to do so, and now the moment was past.

She glanced at Margaret, and again she had the impulse to be kind to someone who was grieving for the same cause as herself.

"I'm genuinely sorry that it – it turned out like this for you," she said hesitatingly. "But I think you must be mistaken about his being in love with you, because, after all, he did marry me." That came a little more confidently, because she supposed there must be *some* sort of truth in it. Leaving out all question of his feelings towards herself, he would hardly have married her – or anyone else – for the flimsy reason he had, if he was already desperately in love with this girl.

"You don't understand." Margaret twitched her shoulder impatiently.

"I'm afraid I don't," Valerie confessed. "But I wish you'd be a little more frank. This – this business of his passing you off as his sister, for instance. Please do tell me when he first suggested the idea to you, and – and what explanation he gave."

Margaret looked at her rather blankly for a moment, and Valerie thought, "She's really rather a stupid girl, for all her brightness and sparkle when she is interested."

"When did he first suggest the idea?" Margaret repeated slowly. Then she seemed to gather her thoughts together more. "Oh, not – not very long ago. It was – it was –" she hesitated.

"A harmless way of meeting," suggested Valerie rather crisply.

"Exactly." There was a slight pause, while Margaret watched Valerie with the only hint of anxiety she had ever shown regarding the reactions of Nigel's wife. "You *must* know that these – these rush marriages nearly always pall very quickly. I'm sorry – but that's the brutal fact. I'm sorry if the 'sister' story makes you unhappy" – she was much more confident now – "but he could hardly have had me here, where all his colleagues are, unless – well, unless there was some sort of explanation."

Valerie didn't comment on that. She was watching the other girl closely. On the whole, she was pretty certain that Margaret was not being quite truthful. But in that case, what *was* the real truth?

"What made you say that about – about Nigel marrying me in a hurry?" She hated herself for continuing the discussion, but she *had* to try to find out a little more.

"Well, he did marry you in a hurry, didn't he?" Margaret's gaze was full on her, with an innocent expression which, Valerie felt sure, was not quite genuine.

"Yes, I suppose you could call it that. But did he – tell you about it?"

Margaret nodded.

"*What* did he tell?"

"Well, that – that one sometimes did these things on impulse, and – I'm sorry – regretted them afterwards."

"That's not true," Valerie said coldly and with absolute conviction. Whatever Nigel had *thought,* she knew positively that he would never have *said* such a thing.

Margaret shrugged.

"I didn't expect you to like it," she said.

"You were foolish to expect me to believe it," Valerie told her shortly. "It's just about as uncharacteristic of Nigel as it could be."

Margaret didn't answer that. She looked faintly sulky, and as though she were not very much interested in what Valerie was saying.

"Listen" – in her eagerness Valerie leant forward and put her hand on the other girl's arm – "there's something very – horrid about misrepresenting Nigel's actions when he's not here. Don't you see it? You haven't told me quite the truth, have you? Please remember that Nigel is missing – that he may be dead – we've got to face that fact. You don't want to sit there telling me things that will make me think of him in a wrong light, do you? He – he can't defend himself, you see."

For a moment Margaret's expression changed. The rather hard, bright resolution wavered, and Valerie thought she was going to get at the truth at last.

"*I* love Nigel too," she said quietly. "The only thing is to let him choose, when the time comes, according to the *true* state of affairs."

But she saw at once that her admission had shut the door on any possible confidences of Margaret's. She got to her feet quickly, almost brushing Valerie's hand from her arm.

"There's nothing else to say. I suppose no wife likes to hear that her husband is in love with someone else, and it's much the easiest way out to pretend that she thinks it a lie. I – I've nothing else to say to you about it. I've told you *my* part of the story. You must take it or leave it, just as you like."

She didn't actually look at Valerie while she was saying all this. Instead, she busied herself fastening her coat and pulling on her gloves. Valerie watched her without a word. Only when her visitor was quite ready she spoke.

"I'm sorry. As you say, there's nothing else to be done about it. Good-bye."

"Good-bye." Margaret seemed half inclined to hold out her hand, thought better of it and, even humming a little to herself – perhaps to show her own assurance – she went out of the room, closing the door after her.

For a minute or two after she had gone, Valerie stood where she was in the middle of the room. Then, with a sigh, she sat down in the chair which Margaret had left.

She was no further forward. She knew nothing more reassuring. There was still not a thing she could do but wait and wait and wait – until there was some news.

Now she could not imagine why she had been so ridiculous as not to ask him outright what the explanation was. It seemed such a simple idea – now that she could no longer put it into effect. Why hadn't she just said quite frankly:

"I don't think there's anything very sisterly about Margaret, and I happened to see you greet her as someone you already knew. Do tell me what the mystery is?"

But she had let the precious chances slip by, and now they might not come again.

Valerie was just wondering aimlessly what else she could do to fill in the long, lonely afternoon, when once more the chambermaid came knocking at the door.

"Mrs. Hanson, there's a lady to see you again."

"Again? Do you mean she's come back?"

"No, ma'am. It's another lady. Quite a different kind of lady. Not very smart, and worried like."

"To see me? Are you sure? I can't imagine who would even know I was here."

"She said it was you she wanted,' the maid insisted, and Valerie, supposing it was the wife of one of Nigel's colleagues, asked for her to be brought upstairs.

But when the door opened again, it was not to admit any stranger. Into the room came Cousin Susan – for once without Gerald – and obviously full of anxiety and self-pity.

"Oh, Valerie, *here* you are!" she exclaimed "I've had such a business to find you. What a *very* pokey little room."

"I'm sorry you don't like the room." Valerie suppressed a smile. "But what is it, Susan? What can I do for you?"

"Oh, Valerie, I do *hope* you'll do it." Susan spoke with great earnestness. "I want you to come right back home with me to Monks Alder."

"You want me to come back to Monks Alder?" Valerie repeated slowly. "But, Susan, why?" She couldn't resist adding, "You've hardly moved back there yourself," a remark Susan ignored. "When would you want me to come?"

"Oh, right away, Val. There isn't anything to prevent you, is there?" Susan could not imagine anyone having plans which interfered with her own. "Gerald won't be there for another few days. I told him I was sure you would come back with me."

Valerie hesitated, then sighed, "Very well, Susan." She was conscious of a sudden sick regret in leaving the place. It seemed, somehow, the only real link she had with Nigel, and now that was snapping. Perhaps she had been silly to decide to leave. And yet what was there to be done by staying?

No, better go back to Monks Alder and try to pick up what threads she could from her old life. She *had* to fill in the dreadful gap some way, and she would do it best in the dear, familiar surroundings of her real home.

CHAPTER XI

It was very, very good to be home, and even Susan's presence could not take away from the pleasure of it. Certainly she was much easier to live with when Gerald was not there, and if she was neither warm-hearted nor a cheering companion, at least she interfered very little with the small pleasures which had always made up Valerie's life at Monks Alder.

Most of the time, Valerie still felt numb. There was still no news of Nigel; an all-out air-sea-rescue operation had so far found nothing.

Two or three days after her return, Valerie met Mr. Ward in the village. She was passing his office just as he was entering it, and he invited her in, with something approaching cordiality.

"I have just heard from your husband," he informed her almost cheerfully, "and I —"

"Heard from Nigel!" Valerie paused with her hand on the back of the chair he had put forward, her lips parted, and the colour draining from her face.

"Certainly. Are you surprised?" Mr. Ward adjusted his indoor spectacles and regarded Valerie with some astonishment. "The letter was waiting for me when I came back here yesterday after having been away for a few days."

"Oh — I — see." The explanation was perfectly simple after all, but the disappointment was so bitter that

Valerie suffered actual physical pain.

It had been absurd to suppose Mr. Ward *could* have had any news of him, only –

Rather slowly Valerie sat down in the chair Mr. Ward had offered, but even bending her head failed to hide the fact that she was in tears.

"My dear lady!" Mr. Ward was most genuinely distressed, and polished his spectacles again as though that might enable him to see something less disturbing. "I am very sorry to have upset you like this, but I don't quite understand."

"N – no, of course not – please forgive me for being so silly. Only, you see, Nigel is missing, and when you said you had heard from him, I thought – It was ridiculous of me. Of course, I see now. He wrote to you some days ago and the letter has been waiting here for you." She explained about the missing plane.

"Precisely." Mr. Ward could not quite keep himself from looking up the letter to verify the date, but, having done that, he regarded Valerie with a really kindly glance. "I am very sorry indeed about your husband," he said sincerely. "I hope you have some reason to think there is still hope."

"I'm hoping so." Valerie was quite calm again now. "One *must* go on hoping that unless there – there is something more definite."

"Certainly, certainly." Mr. Ward was about to add that while there was life there was hope, but, recollecting that this hardly applied in the present case, he tried another tack. "I am pleased to say that your husband instructed me to act for him in the matter of the disputed estate."

"Oh, did he? I'm so glad! I know he meant to, but I wasn't sure if he had actually written about it."

"Yes." The lawyer seemed gratified by her approval. "Though, of course," he added gravely, "the position has now changed somewhat. I am not sure how this latest development affects the question. Your husband" – Valerie had an uneasy feeling that his passion for exactitude made him want to add "or late husband" – "your husband has not yet been officially presumed killed, I take it?"

"No – I don't think so," Valerie said rather faintly.

"Then for the purposes of the law, he is *not* yet – dead, and I shall continue to carry out his instructions."

"Yes, please do," Valerie agreed eagerly. "What do you propose to do about it, Mr. Ward?"

He seemed a good deal more communicative than on the last occasion she had tackled him, and with a slight, dry smile, he informed her:

"I have already opened the case, as a matter of fact. I have only just now come back from Town, where I have been seeing the representative of Messrs. Foster & Foster. You will remember that they are acting for –"

"Yes, yes, I know. They're Gerald's solicitors."

Mr. Ward inclined his head.

"And what did they say?"

"Well –" Mr. Ward appeared to draw the line at giving a verbatim report, but distinct satisfaction showed in his manner. "It is a little early to express a definite opinion, but I must say I have gained the impression that this – this young woman's story is exceedingly thin, and that no one is more aware of the fact than Messrs. Foster & Foster."

"Oh!" Valerie gazed at him thoughtfully, trying to decide just where this new fact fitted into the puzzle. "You mean even Foster & Foster think Margaret – the so-called sister, I mean – knows Nigel isn't her brother?"

"Oh, whether she *knows* it or not is a different matter. She may be honestly of the opinion that he is, or she may, for reasons of her own, merely be asserting that he is. I could only tell that after interviewing the lady herself." Valerie could not help thinking that even an interview with Margaret might well leave Mr. Ward still in considerable doubt. "The point is, however, that the evidence supporting her assertion is of the flimsiest."

"Is it?" Valerie was interested.

"Of the flimsiest," repeated Mr. Ward, as though even now he could hardly credit the fact that anyone had even put it forward. "It rests almost entirely on an extremely incomplete diary kept by her late mother and containing, so far as I can judge, references which could only be called most inconclusive."

"Then why did a firm like Foster & Foster even take up the case?" Valerie couldn't help asking.

"Well" – Mr. Ward took off his spectacles and balanced them delicately in the manner of a famous judge for whom he had an ardent, though concealed, admiration – "consider the position, Mrs. Hanson. Your cousin – Mr. Manders, that is to say – had already informed them that he wished to dispute the claim of your husband to the late Mrs. Hanson's estate. At that identical time they receive a visit from a young woman claiming to be your husband's sister and asking for his present address. However improbable her story appeared, they could naturally do nothing but communicate with their client who, if I may say so, probably seized upon the situation with – er – enthusiasm."

"I see." Valerie bit her lip. She did see – so far as Mr. Ward had outlined the facts. But she wished passionately that she could see just a little further.

At any rate, it seemed that this fantastic scheme of passing Margaret off as Nigel's sister had originated with Margaret herself. That he had accepted the situation was undeniable, but – Valerie's heart lightened – it was no longer so obvious that he had set out to deceive her. In fact, his surprise at Margaret's appearance began to be more understandable now. He had been astonished that the mysterious sister *had turned out to be someone he already knew*.

Valerie's rising spirits received something of a check as she re-faced the fact that he *had* already known Margaret and concealed the fact. But Mr. Ward interrupted her thoughts before she could pursue that further.

"Am I to understand that you are back at Monks Alder, Mrs. Hanson, and that you will be making your home there indefinitely?"

"Yes. At least for the time being. I'm staying there with Susan – with Mrs. Manders, you know."

"Mrs. Manders!" Mr. Ward forgot his impersonation of the judge and placed his spectacles back upon his nose once more. "But what, may I ask, is she doing there?"

"Oh well, you see, she and Gerald think it is as good as proved that Nigel is an impostor, and I'm afraid they have planted themselves back there again – at least, I mean, Susan has. Gerald is away on business. I haven't quite enough claim to turn her out again, and I suppose – come to that – she could hardly turn me out either. But, in any case, she has asked me to go back there for the time being. She is quite able to ignore any little thing like my marriage if it suits her, and, for my part, I must own that I am very glad to be back at Monks Alder, whatever the reason."

"Most irregular!" ejaculated Mr. Ward.

"Is it?" Valerie was amused.

"Why, of course!" He regarded her severely. "I never heard of a precedent for such a position. Both parties residing in the property under dispute. Quite, quite irregular."

"I don't know that it really matters," Valerie said with a slight sigh. "It happens to suit us both, Mr. Ward. And, anyway, the whole case is a bit ridiculous, isn't it?" She reflected that any case so closely connected with Susan and Gerald was almost bound to have an element of the ridiculous about it.

Mr. Ward, however, deprecated the word, much preferring his own choice of "irregular." But, seeing that he was likely to repeat it yet again, Valerie interrupted hastily.

"I think you had better know just how much I discovered – and didn't discover – while I was in London," she said, and proceeded to give him a short account of Nigel's own story and of Margaret's appearance. After a moment's hesitation, she even added a laconic "post-script" describing Margaret's visit to herself and her admission that she was not really Nigel's sister.

"She *admitted* as much?" Mr. Ward was scandalised. "Most extraordinary! Then what was her object in making her original assertion?"

"I don't know. I suppose I'd better tell you," Valerie added grimly, "that she claims that she and my husband are in love with each other. They met a year ago in Canada, according to her."

"Hm." Mr. Ward glanced at her shrewdly. "And what was your impression?"

"About her?"

"Well, about the possibility of this young woman and your husband being – being attached to one another."

"I should say she was infatuated with him."

"And he?"

Almost for the first time, Valerie dispassionately reviewed Nigel's attitude towards Margaret.

"He found her amusing and – Well, no," Valerie admitted with considerable surprise. "I don't think Nigel ever did give the impression of being in love with her."

"He would naturally have endeavoured to conceal the fact in front of you."

"Yes, but it isn't only that." Valerie leant forward with her arm on the desk in interest at her discovery and her eagerness to make herself clear. "I realise now – he took it all much too lightly and amusedly, if you know what I mean. He did know her – I'm sure of that, but –"

"Then the story about their meeting in Canada is quite probably correct."

"Yes, I think it is, but –"

"Otherwise his attitude was that of a man who was amused by, and a little admiring of, a rather daring escapade?"

Valerie looked at the elderly lawyer with a new respect.

"Mr. Ward, I think you're right."

"I should like," Mr. Ward remarked, "to have a talk with this young woman."

"I'd love you to!" Valerie agreed with slightly uncharitable fervour.

Mr. Ward gave his wintry smile which could, however, express a good deal of private amusement.

"It may be possible. Meanwhile, Mrs. Hanson, if I may say so—"

"Yes?"

"I should not attach overwhelming importance to anything this young woman said."

"Oh, I shouldn't."

"But you felt a little natural uneasiness?"

"Well —" Valerie flushed. "I – I still don't know quite why Nigel didn't explain things to me if it was just some silly escapade."

"In front of her?"

"At least when she had gone."

"Hm." Mr. Ward did his impersonation of the judge again. "Was there ample opportunity for explanation, or —"

Valerie's expression told him the answer. Her colour deepened still further, and she looked ashamed and contrite.

"No, I hadn't thought of that. I didn't give – I mean, there wasn't much opportunity. In fact – I think I've been rather a fool, one way and another."

"A common human failing," the lawyer assured her kindly if sententiously.

"But rather humiliating when one finds it applies to oneself." Valerie laughed and made a little face.

But how wonderful it was to be *able* to laugh again! To feel a certain lightness of heart in spite of all the anxiety – a definite hope that, even if Nigel had no specially deep love for her, at least it was unlikely that he had been either deceiving her or making a fool of her.

"Does the – er – prospect look a little brighter?" Mr. Ward inquired with his dry smile again.

"If *only* Nigel is still alive, I think – I could – imagine that everything might come right one day. Anyway, I feel much happier now than when I came into your office."

"My dear," Mr. Ward said – and he seemed to forget about adding "Mrs. Hanson" that time – "I'm extremely glad to hear it."

Valerie shook hands with him very warmly before she took her leave. And as she walked rather slowly back to Monks Alder, she reflected how extraordinarily human the most unlikely people could become in a crisis.

When Valerie came in, she went into the lounge, where she found Susan sitting at the writing-desk, where Aunt Evelyn had so often sat, reading a letter, and, at the same time, sucking the top of her fountain pen with that concentration which always preceded one of her specially incoherent outpourings on paper.

"Hello, Susan. Writing letters?" Valerie asked absently, more for something to say than anything else. But at the slightly guilty start her cousin gave, she immediately became amusedly interested.

"Well, I was *going* to write a letter," Susan explained.

"Don't let me put you off your stroke," Valerie smiled, and, picking up her knitting, she sat down in a chair by the fire. At the silence, however, she glanced up again, and could not resist adding, "You're not writing to any-one Gerald doesn't know about, are you?"

"Val! How can you suggest such a thing!" Susan always took these matters very literally. "Certainly *not*. In fact, Gerald himself has suggested I should write. Only – Val, I want to be *quite* frank with you" – Susan evidently wished to be nothing of the sort – "I hope you won't feel *upset* or – or uncomfortable about it. But I propose to invite Miss Allen down here for a week-end."

"Margaret Allen?" Valerie looked astounded.

"Yes." Susan became firmer. "The sister of – of – well, you know who. Gerald says" – she consulted the letter in her hand – "Gerald says it might be better for *all* of us if we get to the bottom of this sad business."

"I'm not at all upset or uncomfortable about it," she assured Susan gravely. "Only I can't quite see why you think that will help. I should have thought you would have left all the – well, the interviewing and investiga-tion to your lawyers."

Susan looked uncomfortable again, but sought sup-port from Gerald's letter once more.

"Gerald says," she explained firmly, "that a *frank* and sympathetic discussion with this girl should help us to reach the truth."

"I see." Valerie's mouth hardened suddenly. She saw now just what was in Gerald's mind. He had heard from Susan, of course, that Nigel was safely out of the way, and he considered it a golden opportunity for "get-ting at" the so-called sister. It was really typical Gerald technique.

"Do you think she'll come, Susan?" Valerie regarded her cousin with innocent interest.

"I'm *sure* she will. Why shouldn't she?" Susan turned back to the desk and began to write. "After all, I am the only *real* relative belonging to Aunt Evelyn left. She'll probably be pleased and flattered at the idea of getting into direct touch with me."

Valerie silently reviewed what she knew of Margaret, and failed to imagine her flattered by any form of notice from Susan.

"I think it will be very interesting if she does come," she finally murmured with deceptive meekness.

During the next few days, Valerie found an opportunity to tell Mr. Ward that Margaret had actually been invited to Monks Alder by Susan, and was a good deal amused by his dry comment that "if fate were indeed blind, it would at least appear that she occasionally recovered the sight of one eye."

"You will come up to Monks Alder while she is there, won't you, Mr. Ward?"

"Certainly, if I am invited."

"Well, of course *I* invite you now, and I'll let you know the best time to turn up. That is, if she does come," Valerie added a little dubiously.

"Oh, she will come." On that point at least Mr. Ward and Susan appeared to be at one.

Valerie looked amused.

"Why are you so sure?"

"Because she has no idea that you are here, and if she is as – interested in your husband as you suppose, she will certainly not neglect an opportunity of coming in touch with his relations – so-called or otherwise."

" 'So-called or otherwise' is about the right description," Valerie remarked with a laugh. "It's difficult sometimes to remember who is a relation and who isn't in this tangle."

"Well, at least there is no doubt about your relationship to Mr. Hanson," the lawyer reminded her. And he went off, leaving Valerie to reflect that, in his own way, Mr. Ward had a considerable sense of humour.

When Margaret arrived, Valerie was not in the house. She had gone down to the village to fetch something for which Susan had suddenly evinced an urgent need. Knowing her cousin's tactics, Valerie thought it not unlikely that she was being got out of the way on purpose, but as this in no way interfered with her own plans, she raised no objection.

"I wish I could know for certain that she would be there when I get back," thought Valerie.

And then fate – possibly recovering a little more sight – suddenly played straight into her hands. As Valerie came out of the village store, the one decrepit taxi which the village boasted chugged past her up the hill. She had one glimpse of the inmate, but one glimpse was sufficient. She would have known that huge scarlet hat anywhere.

Margaret had arrived.

In quite unnecessary anxiety lest she should be noticed, Valerie stepped back abruptly into the doorway of the shop, and when the taxi had passed, she set off for Mr. Ward's office at something little less than a run.

"Mr. Ward!" Valerie hurried into his room, holding out her hands. "She's here!" Then, feeling that was perhaps unnecessarily dramatic, she added, "Margaret Allen. I've just seen her drive up to Monks Alder in the taxi. Could you possibly, possibly come back with me now? Please do. I'm sure the right thing is to confront her with us both as soon as possible."

Rising with a briskness which did him credit, Mr. Ward thrust the papers before him into a drawer with the nearest thing to a lack of ceremony that Valerie had ever seen in him. He changed his indoor spectacles for his outdoor ones with a hand that trembled slightly, making Valerie wonder if he could possibly be genuinely excited. Then, reaching for his hat and coat, he spoke for the first time.

"I think," he said, "we are ready for the young woman."

As they passed through the outer office, an anguished glance from the junior clerk strove to ascertain whether Valerie had indeed betrayed his lapse. But the absorption of them both in something other than his unworthy self restored his confidence and his self-esteem, and even his interest in his crossword puzzle.

It was not a long walk to Monks Alder, and Valerie and the lawyer said little to each other on the way. She only paused to remark once:

"Of course I just – met you quite casually, and thought it would be very kind of you to drop in to tea."

"Of course, of course," Mr. Ward agreed a little testily, as though the explanation were so self-evident that it was foolish even to mention it.

At Monks Alder Valerie, her chin tilted a trifle defiantly, led the way into the lounge where Susan was rather effusively entertaining her visitor to tea.

"Oh, Val" – Susan rose to her feet, divided between triumph and nervousness. "This is Miss Allen. Miss Allen, this is your – um – brother's solicitor. And, Mr.

Ward, this is the sister of – of the so-called Mr. Hanson."

"But I thought" – Valerie looked with friendly puzzlement at the astounded Margaret – "I thought when I last saw you that you told me Nigel was *not* your brother."

"When you last saw her!" Susan repeated with a dismay that was ludicrous. "But you've *never* seen her before, Val."

"Oh yes, once or twice." Valerie smilingly took the reluctant hand which Margaret had not even extended to her. "Nigel introduced us. How are you, Margaret? I was hoping you would find time to come to Monks Alder."

"But – but you never *told* me." Susan gazed at Valerie with indignant reproach. "Valerie, how *deceitful* of you. I think you're just as bad as that man – I'm sorry, Miss Allen, but your brother was – was always impersonating people," Susan added, allowing herself a little poetic licence. "It's so confusing, and –"

"There seems," observed Mr. Ward, removing his glasses and substituting his other pair, the better to regard Margaret – "there seems to be a certain amount of confusion regarding this young lady's own identity. Perhaps she will help us. Do I understand that you are indeed Miss Allen? – Miss Margaret Allen?"

"Yes, of course." Margaret tossed her head. "I don't know where the confusion is. I've never pretended to be anyone but Margaret Allen."

"No," agreed Mr. Ward. "Perhaps it would have been more accurate if I had said that you – inadvertently or otherwise" – and he gave Margaret a singularly steely look – "cast doubts on the identity of someone else."

"I don't see why *I* should be catechised by people," Margaret exclaimed indignantly. "I thought I had come down here on a visit of pleasure" – she shot a spiteful glance at Susan which caused that lady to bridle – "but it seems more like walking into a court of law."

"I can assure you," Mr. Ward told her smoothly, "that this scene has no resemblance whatsoever to a court of law. And," he added as an afterthought, "we all hope your visit will be one of pleasure. But I am sure you will not refuse to assist us in a matter which has caused us all a good deal of anxiety and worry."

He paused, and, after a moment, Margaret said, "Well?" rather sulkily.

Mr. Ward smiled, as though he were not particularly surprised to receive this somewhat ungracious permission to proceed.

"I think you met Mr. Hanson first something over a year ago, when you were both living in Montreal."

Margaret nodded.

"You became quite friendly –"

"Very friendly," Margaret insisted with an unkind glance this time at Valerie.

"Very friendly," repeated Mr. Ward equably. "But – ah – not to the extent of exchanging addresses when you parted."

Margaret gave him a startled look.

"How did you – Well, I lost his address, anyway," she said. "What does that matter?"

"It doesn't matter at all," Mr. Ward assured her smoothly. "These things are so easily mislaid. But *after* you had parted from Mr. Hanson, something he had said about his going to Canada when he was a child made you connect him in your mind with your own journey there."

"I don't know what all this has to do with you."

"I am only seeking to explain how you hit on the very ingenious method of coming back into Mr. Hanson's life in circumstances that would intrigue and interest him."

"Oh" – Margaret made an impatient gesture – "you seem to know all about it. I'm sick of the whole thing myself. It was mostly just for fun anyway."

"It is never fun, Miss Allen," Mr. Ward informed her, "to endeavour to deceive people."

"But I don't under*stand,*" poor Susan interrupted.

"I think I do." Valerie was rather pale. "All the part about the – the plane crash and the diary is quite true. Only even you yourself never believed that there had been any confusion about the two boys. But the disjointed diary was useful, and, armed with that, you could go to the solicitors dealing with Aunt Evelyn's affairs –"

"Pardon me. *I* was dealing with your aunt's affairs," Mr. Ward interrupted firmly.

"Well – yes. I'm sorry. The solicitors acting for one of Aunt Evelyn's heirs, and find out just where Nigel was, and turn up in his life again in circumstances that were bound to interest him and perhaps – perhaps touch him."

"A *most* improper proceeding," commented Mr. Ward.

"But" – Valerie felt suddenly sorry for Margaret, who looked so sullen and chagrined – "but rather understandable."

Mr. Ward looked astounded, evidently not finding it at all understandable.

"At least" – Valerie amended a little guiltily – "I *can* imagine someone doing it more or less for – for a lark. That was it, wasn't it, Margaret?" She suddenly very much wanted to save the self-respect of this girl who was fond of Nigel in her way but had tried so unscrupulously to attach herself to him. "You – you didn't even mean to keep the pretence up for long, once you'd seen him?"

Margaret shrugged – a little relieved, Valerie thought.

"No. I expect the truth would have come out pretty soon, and we'd have laughed over it together, instead of everyone having heroics and talking like the Last Judgment," she added with an unfriendly glance at Mr. Ward.

"The only difficulty was that you – you hadn't thought of his getting married in the year when you had lost sight of him?"

"Well, of course, that did complicate things a bit."

"Then do you mean" – Susan got in a word at last – "you *can't* mean – that this Nigel Hanson person *is* Nigel Hanson."

"Yes, of course." Margaret looked at her with open contempt. "Does it matter?"

"Matter?" repeated poor Susan as the full results of this frank and sympathetic discussion dawned upon her. *"Matter?* Why, it means that Monks Alder belongs to him, after all! And if he's dead, it belongs to *Val!"* And she began to cry.

"Oh, my goodness!" Margaret exclaimed. "Is this a

madhouse? Anyway, I don't expect any of you are too anxious to have me stay here any longer, and I've an idea I can have a more amusing week-end somewhere else. I'm sorry, Mrs. Manders, if you don't like what you've heard, but I won't stay and tell you any more."

As though the place belonged to her, she marched out into the hall – almost knocking over Mabel, who "happened" to be reprehensibly near the door.

"Will you get me a taxi, please," she said curtly.

"There is only one," Mabel informed her, just as curtly. "But I'll telephone for that."

She did so, with more speed than she had shown over any operation for many a long day. And after an uneasy interval of ten minutes, the ancient taxi came chugging up the drive.

Margaret showed little desire for prolonged farewells, and no one sought to detain her. As Mabel closed the door behind her, Valerie held out her hand to Mr. Ward, and very gravely they exchanged a hearty handshake.

"I don't know *what* Gerald will say," Susan said with an injured sigh. "Everyone seems to have behaved *very* deceitfully. I should think you'd feel *very* uncomfortable, having married into such a family, Val."

"You forget," Mr. Ward reminded her coldly, "that this – somewhat unbalanced Miss Allen is not a member of any family into which Mrs. Hanson has married."

"Oh no, of course not. Oh dear, how *terribly* confusing it all is." And Susan went off disconsolately to her room to nurse a nervous headache which, for once, Valerie felt she was justified in pleading.

As she herself walked down the drive later with Mr. Ward, she suddenly slipped her hand into his arm.

"I can't thank you enough, Mr. Ward. You managed it splendidly."

"My dear, I simply recited the facts."

"Yes – but so cleverly. How did you think out what it was she had really done?"

"Merely by giving my undivided attention to the case," Mr. Ward assured her with a smile. "The central fact that your husband was surprised at seeing her arrive in the character of the long-lost sister showed that when they had originally met, she had not yet connected him with the plane crash and her mother's diary. That idea must have come to her later, and – given the kind of young woman she is – one could safely assume that she would use that discovery in an unconventional and even unscrupulous way."

"Ye – es, I suppose so. I wish I'd been half as bright about it all as you have. It – it might have saved a lot of unhappiness."

"I hope the late discovery will serve to provide a lot of happiness at some future date," the lawyer assured her, as he shook hands.

"I hope so," Valerie smiled. "And I – *we* won't forget that we owed it all to you."

She leant her arms on the gate and watched him go off down the lane. He *was* a good sort, as Nigel had said, and he had served their cause remarkably well. It was lucky that he had been "on their side".

She smiled as she remembered how delighted Nigel had been when she had used that expression.

Oh, Nigel! Why wasn't he here to learn of his own vindication? *He* was the rightful owner of dear Monks Alder – and he had never slept there even one night. He had said he wanted her to have the place if anything happened to him. But that was just his dear, absurd, quixotic way. The place belonged to him, and must wait as impatiently as she did until he returned – if ever.

The familiar chill feathered over her heart as she thought of Nigel. For much of the time she had been managing to push the worry into the background of her thoughts – but it wasn't actually very far in the background, and as, nearing the house again, she heard the phone ringing her heart began to pound and she ran into the hall to answer it.

"Mrs. Hanson?" She almost stopped breathing as she recognised the voice of Robert Edwardes, but she managed to say "yes," very faintly. "Mrs. Hanson – it's all right, don't faint or anything, will you? It's Nigel – he's safe!"

CHAPTER XII

"SAFE?" Valerie was laughing and crying at the same
time.

"Yes, Mrs. Hanson. We had a telephone call ten minutes ago. He was picked up in a life-raft by an R.A.F.
rescue plane – there were only two survivors from the
crash, it seems, so it was a miraculous escape. Anyway,
he's home again now."

"What do you mean – he's home again?" Valerie's
voice was shaking with emotion. "Where is he?"

"That's the best part of all, Mrs. Hanson. Apparently
he was in fairly good shape when they picked him up –
apart from a broken arm and the obvious after-effects of
exposure for several days – and somehow, don't ask me
how, he persuaded the R.A.F. to fly him home to U.K.
almost immediately. He's in the R.A.F. hospital at Rad-
dershaw, not fifty miles from you. He –"

But Valerie had put the phone down and flown out
of the house to get the village taxi.

"Well," – the very pretty nurse smiled doubtfully at
Valerie – "of course it's quite against the rules except
when a patient is on the danger list. And, fortunately,
your husband isn't anywhere near that."

"But I've been thinking him dead." Valerie's voice
broke a little in spite of her efforts to steady it. "I only
heard an hour or two ago that he was here, and safe.
And – and anyway, I quarrelled a bit with him just be-

fore he went away. *"Please* can't I see him?"

"I'll ask Sister." The nurse looked sympathetic. "I'll try to make her understand," she added with almost ingenuous fervour, and disappeared behind one of the important-looking doors that lined the short corridor to the ward.

Not daring even to tiptoe to the door of the ward, Valerie stood where she was, watching the big open fire at the end of the long room, and the pinky glow it cast over the many beds with their quiet occupants.

Which of those was Nigel? Was she really within a few yards of him? – within a few minutes of hearing his voice? – or would she have –

"It's all right. Sister says ten minutes only." The nurse was back beside her. "But you can say a lot in ten minutes," she added comfortingly.

Valerie nodded, too much moved and excited to speak, and followed the nurse into the ward.

Somehow she had not expected him to be in the very first bed – but there he was, his bright eyes rather shadowed for once and his big figure singularly still.

He glanced idly at the nurse, and then at the girl with her – and at the sudden change of expression on his face, Valerie knew she would never have any doubts or fears again.

"Val!" He almost whispered her name, and held out his uninjured arm to her.

Valerie had no idea that the nurse was tactfully putting a screen round the bed or that she herself was breaking all rules by sitting down on the bed. She only knew that his arm was round her and that she was crying a little and kissing him all over his face.

"Why, darling!" He returned her kisses, laughing and holding her tightly. "What's the matter? Don't cry like that – your dear little face is all wet! There's nothing to cry about."

"No – no, I know. At least, not now. Now that you're safe. I thought – I thought – Oh, Nigel can I put my arms round you?"

"You bet you can!"

"No, I mean, will it hurt you?"

"No. I shouldn't care if it did."

She slid her arms round him and hugged him.

"Oh, Nigel, I thought I'd lost you."

"And that would have mattered so much?"

"You *know* it would."

He smiled at her and shook his head.

"No, I don't."

"Oh no, of course you didn't know. I – I – Nigel, you do love me, don't you?"

"Like hell."

"That sounds a lot."

"It is. And it hurts."

"Oh, darling, I'm sorry. But it needn't hurt if I love you too, need it?"

"No." He kissed her again. "Not if you love me too."

"I do, Nigel. I've been such a fool – oh, and such an unworthy little beast too, and –"

"No, no." – He laughed and put his cheek against the top of her head. "I won't have anyone talking that way about the girl I love."

"But it's true! I thought –"

"– that I was in love with Margaret?"

"Yes. How did you know?"

"Because you looked jealous, darling – blessedly jealous, for the first time, that day the little idiot turned up."

"Oh, Nigel, wasn't it *small* of me?"

"No. Just stupid of me not to explain at once. But I couldn't in front of her because she'd got her whole silly escapade worked out to her own satisfaction. And then when I came to your room afterwards you didn't seem exactly chatty. I thought, 'I'll explain tomorrow, when it's easier,' but there wasn't any tomorrow. At least, not until now."

"And now – it's all right?" She looked up at him.

"It suits me." He smiled down at her.

"Oh, and it's all right about Monks Alder too. She came down there this afternoon –"

"Who did?"

"Margaret."

"*Did* she?"

"Um-hm. But it didn't matter. Mr. Ward and I saw her, and she had to admit that she knew perfectly well you were no brother of hers, and there was no question about your being anyone but Nigel Hanson, and – oh well, there's nothing else to worry about, except" – she smiled suddenly – "that Susan doesn't quite know what Gerald will say."

Nigel laughed.

"Tell her that I know what he ought to say."

"And that is?"

"The same as he said to you when he wanted to turn you out of Monks Alder. That one person's good fortune is bound to be another person's bad fortune. Kiss me, darling. Life's like that – as Gerald says."

Each month from Harlequin

8 NEW FULL LENGTH ROMANCE NOVELS

Listed below are the latest three months' releases:

ALL BOOKS 60c

These titles are available at your local bookseller, or through the Harlequin Reader Service, M.P.O. Box 707, Niagara Falls, N.Y. 14302; Canadian address 649 Ontario St., Stratford, Ont.

J